"You offered to he
you watch the boy
replacement sitter?"

Babysit? Him? "I don't think that's a good idea."

"It would be for two or three days at the most."

"But I don't know anything about kids."

She ignored his protests. "I'd need you to drop them off at preschool and bring them back here afterward."

"I'm sure—" Conway glanced at the boys "—they'd rather have anyone but me watch them."

"Oh, never mind." Her shoulders sagged.

Hell. How hard could it be to watch a couple of four-year-olds? For two years Isi had listened to him bellyache about women. He couldn't turn his back on her when she needed him most.

"Okay, I'll watch the boys," he said.

She flashed him a bright smile. "You'll need to be here by noon on Monday."

"See you then." Conway couldn't escape fast enough.

Dear Reader,

Twins Under the Christmas Tree is the second book in The Cash Brothers series, and poor Conway Twitty Cash... this man has no idea he's going to fall and fall hard. After tracking down his birth father and learning that he's descended from a long line of cut-'n'-run cowboys, Conway is determined to avoid fatherhood. But now that he's decided to settle down, he can't seem to find a woman who doesn't want children.

Conway's search for *the one* is temporarily interrupted when his friend Isi Lopez asks him to babysit her four-year-old twins. Taking care of her sons isn't hard at all, but seeing Isi each day is rekindling the spark that was between them when they first met—before he discovered Isi was a single mom. When Isi decides she should start dating, Conway sets her up with his brother, believing nothing will happen. Wrong. Conway's brother is showing way too much interest in Isi, and all of a sudden, Conway wants to stake *his* claim on her. But a ready-made family has never been in Conway's plans. Luckily it's Christmastime, because it's going to take a little Santa magic to convince Conway that his happy-ever-after has been right in front of him all this time.

If you missed the first book in The Cash Brothers series, *The Cowboy Next Door* (July 2013) remains available through online retailers. I always enjoy hearing from readers—you can email me at marin@marinthomas.com. You can also find me on Facebook and Twitter, and be sure to check out my Cash Brother Boards on Pinterest. For information on my books, and for my blog, newsletter and monthly contests, please visit www.marinthomas.com.

Happy Ever After...The Cowboy Way!

Marin

TWINS UNDER THE CHRISTMAS TREE

MARIN THOMAS

HARLEQUIN® AMERICAN ROMANCE®

Recycling programs
for this product may
not exist in your area.

ISBN-13: 978-0-373-75473-1

TWINS UNDER THE CHRISTMAS TREE

Copyright © 2013 by Brenda Smith-Beagley

Printed in U.S.A.

www.Harlequin.com

ABOUT THE AUTHOR

Marin Thomas grew up in Janesville, Wisconsin. She left the Midwest to attend college in Tucson, Arizona, where she earned a B.A. in radio-TV. Following graduation she married her college sweetheart in a five-minute ceremony at the historic Little Chapel of the West in Las Vegas, Nevada. Over the years she and her family have lived in seven different states, but they've now come full circle and returned to Arizona, where the rugged desert and breathtaking sunsets provide plenty of inspiration for Marin's cowboy books.

Books by Marin Thomas

HARLEQUIN AMERICAN ROMANCE

The McKade Brothers
*Hearts of Appalachia
*Rodeo Rebels
The Cash Brothers

To my editor Johanna Raisanen—I don't know what I would do without you! I can't thank you enough for the time and care you put into each of my books. I'm probab[ly] one of the few authors who look forward to her editor's revision letter, but I'm always eager to see what ideas and suggestions you have for my stories. Your input and expertise is invaluable, and I'm looking forward to writin[g] many more happy-ever-after tales with you!

Chapter One

Conway Twitty Cash had only one rule when it came to women—never date one with kids. Period. No exceptions. Not even if the woman sent text photos of her hooters.

Friday afternoon at the Midway Arizona Cowboy Rodeo Days, Conway had been the recipient of a sexy text from a buckle bunny he'd met earlier in the day. Once his eyes had quit bugging out at Bridget's voluptuous tatas, he'd noticed a child's Batman cape draped over a chair in the background of the photo. Alarmed, he'd asked his rodeo competitors about Bridget and had learned she was a single mom. When they'd first met, he'd asked if she'd had kids, and she'd said no.

Too upset to focus on his ride, the bronc had tossed him on his head as soon as he cleared the chute. Afterward, Conway had made a beeline for the parking lot—he hadn't been about to wait for Bridget to catch up.

Miffed, ticked off and a whole lotta mad, he pulled into the Border Town Bar & Grill in Yuma—the employer of his good friend and pseudo-therapist Isadora Lopez. Two years ago when he'd first met Isi, he'd been drawn to her dark brown eyes and girl-next-door prettiness. He'd turned on the charm and she'd rewarded his flirting with fleeting touches, accidental bumps and sultry looks. Then he'd asked her to dance during her break and when their bodies had come in contact, a zap of electricity had shot through him. He'd been sure the night would end in Isi's bed, until she'd mentioned that she was a single mother of twin boys.

He'd told Isi that he had nothing against kids, but had no intention of ever being a father. From that day on, they'd settled into a comfortable friendship where Isi listened to his dating adventures and offered advice about how to find the perfect woman—one who didn't want children.

The bar was packed on this late-September afternoon. The crowd sitting in front of the big-screen TV watched a college football game between state rivals the University of Arizona and Arizona State University. Conway slid onto a stool and waved to the barkeep. Red was a mountain of a man—six feet seven inches—and bald with a crimson beard that ended in the middle of his chest.

After handing a pitcher of margaritas to a waitress named Sasha, Red brought Conway a bottle of his favorite beer. "You rodeo today?"

"Got bucked off."

"Too bad."

"Where's Isi?" Conway asked.

"In class." Red checked his watch. "She should be here any minute." Isi was working toward a two-year business degree from the local community college.

Red went to fill a drink order, and Conway picked at the paper label on his beer bottle and silently cursed Bridget. Why was it so difficult to find a woman who didn't want children? After he'd discovered he came from a long line of deadbeat dads, he'd decided he didn't want to follow in their footsteps, but unlike his father, grandfather and great-grandfather Conway wasn't opposed to marriage. He really did want a committed relationship.

He wasn't a braggart, but the face he saw in the mirror each morning had garnered his fair share of female attention. At twenty-eight he'd thought for sure he'd have found "the one" by now, but every time he began thinking happy ever after, "the one" decided she'd like to have children after all.

Maybe he should take a break from his search. He'd been handed the responsibility of managing the family pecan farm, so he had plenty of work to keep his mind off his miserable love life. He lifted the beer bottle to his mouth and knocked his front tooth against the rim when a hand slapped his back. Startled, he spun and came face-to-face with Bridget's tatas.

How the hell had she known where to find him?

She planted her fists on her hips and glared. "Why'd you leave the rodeo after your ride? I thought we were going out on a date."

A date? He'd ended their conversation with "goodbye," not "see you later."

"Howdy, Conway." Sasha winked as she passed him with an empty drink tray.

"Is she special to you?" Bridget dipped her head toward Sasha.

"No."

"Hey, Conway." Isi strolled into the bar, backpack slung over her shoulder.

"What about her?" Bridget asked.

Isi stopped next to the bar and glanced between Conway and Bridget. "What about me what?"

Bridget glared. "Are you and Conway dating?"

"Heck, no."

Conway wasn't sure if he was offended or amused by Isi's fervent denial. It was true they were just friends, but she didn't have to act as if he was the last man on earth she'd consider going out with.

"You're not his type." Bridget gave Isi the once-over.

"Don't insult her," Conway said. Isi might not have been blessed with Bridget's bust size, but her long silky hair and exotic eyes were sexy as heck.

Squinting, Bridget asked, "Are you sure there's nothing going on between you two?"

"Positive." Isi and Conway spoke simultaneously.

"And Conway isn't dating Sasha, because Sasha's a lesbian." Isi's eyes sparkled with mischief.

"Then why'd you stand me up at the rodeo?" Bridget asked.

"I didn't stand you up," Conway said.

Bridget planted her hands on her hips. "You gave me your phone number."

"He gives all the ladies his number," Isi said.

Conway sent his "friend" an I-don't-need-your-help glare.

"You acted like you wanted to see me again." Bridget stuck out her lower lip in a pout.

"I don't date women with children," he said. "Never. Ever. No exceptions."

"Who told you I had a kid?"

"I saw the Batman costume in the picture you texted me."

"That belongs to my nephew."

Isi snickered.

"Get lost," Bridget said.

Isi inched behind Conway. He didn't blame her for being cautious. Bridget was getting really worked up.

"I asked a couple of cowboys about you and they said you had a son."

"I swear he won't get in our way," Bridget said. "I'll make sure he's not there when you visit."

"Sorry, I don't date women with children or women who want children."

"Then why did you lead me on?"

"Hey, I never asked you out on a date. I never promised to call you and I never—"

Bridget cocked her arm and swung. Having grown up defending his name from bullies, Conway's reflexes were sharp. He ducked in the nick of time and Bridget's fist connected with Isi's nose. The blow sent her reeling. Conway dove off the stool and caught her before she crumpled to the floor.

"What the hell is going on!" Red's booming voice bellowed across the bar.

Bridget took one look at the giant man and sprinted for the door.

"I need a towel and ice," Conway said.

"Here." Sasha shoved paper napkins into his hand and he pressed them against Isi's bleeding nose then led her to a chair. "God, Isi, I'm sorry." He swallowed a curse as the skin beneath both her eyes began to bruise.

Red offered a towel packed with ice, and Conway placed it against her nose.

"I can't feel my face," she moaned.

"Hang on, honey." He wiped away the blood then spoke to Red. "I'm taking her to the emergency room." Damn Bridget. Already Isi's petite nose had swollen to the size of a kosher pickle.

He helped Isi to her feet and Sasha handed him Isi's backpack. Isi swayed after taking a step toward the door, so he tucked her against his side and practically carried her out of the bar.

They drove in silence to the hospital. He figured she was hurting pretty bad if she couldn't give him hell about Bridget. He parked in the visitor lot in front of the emergency entrance.

"I don't need to see a doctor. I'll be fine," she said.

"Let the doctor make that call." When he reached for the door handle, she snagged his shirtsleeve.

"I don't have health insurance."

He wasn't surprised. Isi worked part-time at the bar and by law Red didn't have to offer her benefits. "You got punched in the face because of me. I'll take care of the bill." It was the least he could do.

Once inside, Isi filled out the paperwork then waited almost an hour before a nurse took her to get an X-ray. Conway spoke to a billing representative and made arrangements to pay for Isi's E.R. visit. By the time Isi returned to the waiting room, the bruising beneath her eyes had worsened.

"A clean fracture," the nurse announced. She handed Conway a bottle of pain pills. "No driving while she's taking this prescription."

Conway shoved the container into his jean pocket, thanked the nurse and escorted Isi to his truck. "Do you have a concussion?"

"No."

"Want to take a pain pill right now? I'll go back inside and buy you a bottle of water from the vending machine."

"No, thanks. I'll take a pill after I drive myself home."

"You're not driving anywhere tonight."

"I can't leave my car at Red's."

Conway didn't want to pick a fight with Isi when she was hurting. He drove her to the bar and parked next to her 1996 white Toyota Camry. "I'll follow you to your place."

"That's not necessary."

"Maybe, but I'll feel better knowing you got home safe."

She grabbed her backpack then hopped out and slammed the truck door. Conway drove behind her as she pulled out of the lot. He knew she lived in a trailer park nearby but had forgotten which one.

Isi headed southwest a mile then entered the Desert Valley Mobile Home Park. The neighborhood was well kept—mostly single wides. She pulled beneath a carport in front of a white trailer with faded turquoise trim. Instead of the traditional rock and cactus landscape, the yard consisted of dead grass and dirt. He parked behind Isi and followed her to the door.

"Thank you for taking care of the hospital bill," she said.

"I'll pay for any follow-up doctor visits."

"As long as your girlfriends stay away from the bar, I won't need to see any more doctors."

"I'm really sorry. I didn't think Bridget would follow me after I left the rodeo."

"You might have to compromise if you want to find the perfect woman, Conway."

He didn't want to discuss his love life. "Do you have a friend who will stay with you tonight?"

"I'll be fine."

When Isi opened the door, he heard a female talking. "Who's that?"

"The sitter. She's always on her cell phone."

Conway followed Isi inside.

"Oh, my God, what happened?" The teen's eyes widened in horror.

"I'm fine, Nicole." Isi sent Conway a silent message. "I ran into the kitchen door at the bar."

So she didn't want the sitter to know the truth—fine by him, because the truth made him look like an idiot.

"Conway, this is Nicole. She watches the boys when I'm at the bar. Nicole, this is Conway. He's a friend."

"Nice to meet you," Nicole said.

While Isi asked the sitter how the boys had behaved, Conway studied the furnishings. *Sparse* was the first word that came to mind. The furniture appeared secondhand—TV, love seat, chair and coffee table. Kids' artwork decorated the walls and colorful plastic bins filled with toys had been stacked in the living room corner.

"What time did the boys go to bed?" Isi asked.

"Fifteen minutes ago."

"I'm sorry to have to cut the night short." Isi faced Conway. "Where are those pain pills?"

He handed her the bottle and she went into the kitchen and got a drink of water. "I won't be working at the bar this weekend, so I'll see you on Monday, Nicole." Isi disappeared down the hallway then a moment later he heard a door open and close.

"Do you need a ride home, Nicole?" Conway asked.

"No, I live here in the trailer park with my aunt." She walked to the door. "I left a note on the kitchen table for Isi. Will you make sure she reads it in the morning?"

"Sure."

After Nicole left, Conway stood in living room uncertain what to do. Was it okay to leave Isi and her kids alone after she'd taken a pain pill? What if a burglar tried to break into the trailer or the water heater caught on fire? Isi was in no shape to handle a crisis.

The least he could do after she'd taken a blow meant for him was stay the night and make sure she and her sons remained safe. As soon as she woke in the morning, he'd hightail it back to the farm.

A SIXTH SENSE told Conway he was being watched. He opened his eyes beneath the cowboy hat covering his face. Two pairs of miniature athletic shoes stood side by side next to the sofa. He played possum—not an easy task when his legs were numb from dangling over the end of the love seat all night.

"Is he dead?"

The question went unanswered.

"I bet he's dead." The same voice spoke again.

"Poke him and see." A second voice, slightly higher in pitch than the first, whispered.

Conway grinned, glad the hat hid his face.

"Get Mom."

"She's sleeping."

The sound of a food wrapper crinkling reached Conway's ears.

"Shh."

"I'm hungry." Crunching followed the statement.

Conway shifted on the couch and groaned.

"He's alive."

"Maybe he's sick."

"Look under his hat."

"You look."

"Chicken."

"Am not."

Conway's chest shook with laughter as he waited for his assailants' next move. Small fingers lifted the brim of his hat and Cheerio breath puffed against in his face.

On the count of three. *One…two…three.* Conway

opened his eyes and his gaze clashed with the boys'. The kids shrieked and jumped back, bumping into each other. The Cheerio box sailed through the air, the contents spilling onto Conway's chest. He studied the mess then turned his attention to the daring duo.

"Sorry, mister." The brothers scooped oat rings off of Conway's shirt and stuffed them back into the box. Conway swung his legs to the floor and sat up. The twins were identical. They wore their hair cut in a traditional little-boy style with a side part and both had their mother's almond-shaped brown eyes.

He pointed to the kid holding the cereal box. "What's your name?"

"Javier."

Conway moved his finger to the other boy.

"I'm Miguel. Who are you?"

So Miguel was the outgoing one and Javier the shy one. "Conway Twitty Cash."

"That's a long name," Miguel said.

"You can call me Conway." It wasn't enough that his mother had slept with every Tom, Dick and Harry across southern Arizona, but she'd also possessed a strange sense of humor in naming all six of her sons after country-music legends. "How old are you guys?"

"Four." They answered in unison.

"Are you a real cowboy?" Miguel asked.

"That depends. You asking if I work on a ranch?"

Miguel nodded.

"I'm not that kind of cowboy."

Javier made eye contact with his brother and Conway swore the boys conversed telepathically. "What kind of cowboy are you?" Miguel asked.

"Part-time rodeo cowboy. When I'm not bustin' broncs, I work on a farm."

The boys stared with blank expressions.

"You know what pecans are, don't you?"

They shook their heads.

"Nuts that grow on trees. People eat the nuts or use them in pies."

Javier whispered in his brother's ear then Miguel asked, "How come you're in our house?"

Not sure what answer Isi would want him to give her sons, he asked a question of his own. "Have you ever seen a man in your house after you woke up in the morning?"

They shook their heads again.

For some stupid reason that pleased Conway.

Javier whispered in his brother's ear.

"You can ask me questions yourself, Javier," Conway said.

"I mostly talk." Miguel's chest puffed up. "Why are you sleeping on our couch?"

"Your mom wasn't feeling well, so I stayed the night in case something bad happened."

"Is Mom dying?" Miguel paused, then said, "Like what?"

"No, your mom isn't dying. For Pete's sake!" Conway had trouble following the conversation—he'd never talked with four-year-olds before. "Like what, what?"

"What kind of bad things?" Miguel asked.

"Well, there could have been a fire in the middle of the night."

Javier ran from the room then returned with a small fire extinguisher.

"We know how to put out a fire," Miguel said.

He doubted the boys had the strength to pull the pin on the extinguisher, but he was impressed that they knew what the canister was used for. "Or a bad guy could've broken into the trailer."

Javier set down the extinguisher then opened the closet door in the hallway and removed a baseball bat, which he dragged across the carpet. Conway got the impression the kid was trying to tell him that they didn't need his help protecting their mother.

"Can you lift that?" he asked.

Javier raised the bat and Conway intercepted the barrel before it hit Miguel in the back of the head. "Whoa, slugger." He confiscated the weapon and laid it on the couch.

"Javi...Mig... Where are you guys?" Isi's sluggish voice rang out a moment before she appeared in the hallway. Conway sucked in a quiet breath. The bruising beneath her eyes had deepened to dark purple.

"Mom!" Miguel dashed across the room, Javier following him. "What happened?" Both boys hugged Isi's legs.

"I had an accident at work last night. I ran into a door and broke my nose."

"Does it hurt?" Miguel asked.

"Yes. Did you have breakfast?" Isi dropped to one knee and hugged her sons. She whispered in Miguel's ear then he went into the kitchen, climbed onto the counter and retrieved two cereal bowls from the cupboard. Javier remained by Isi's side—he was definitely the insecure twin.

"Mom." Miguel set the bowls on the table.

"What?"

"Conway Twitty Cash slept on our couch."

"You can call me Conway."

"*Mr.* Conway," Isi said.

"I told them I stayed last night, because you weren't

feeling well and I needed to be here in case of an emergency."

"We don't need his help, do we, Javi?" Miguel said.

Javier wouldn't look at Conway.

"It was nice of Mr. Conway to stay, but I'm fine now." Isi sent him a time-to-leave look.

Conway stood up and the Cheerios that had gotten caught in the wrinkles of his shirt spilled to the floor. He stepped over the Os to avoid smashing them into the carpet. "Your sitter left this for you last night." He handed her the piece of paper Miguel had pushed aside on the table. "She wanted you to read it first thing in the morning."

While Isi read the note, Conway said, "I'd really like to make it up to you for what happened last night. Is there anything I can—"

Isi glanced up from the note a stunned expression on her face.

"What's wrong?" he asked.

"Nicole quit."

"What?"

"She's moving to Tucson to live with her father."

"When?" Conway asked.

"Today." Isi sighed. "If I don't find a sitter by Monday, I'll have to skip class and I have an exam that day."

"Maybe your mother could help out with the boys."

She frowned. "My mother's dead."

That's right. She'd told him her mother had passed away right before she'd immigrated to the U.S. He inched closer to the door. "Maybe a relative—"

"Conway—"

Hand on the doorknob he froze. "What?"

"I told you a long time ago that I don't have any family. It's just me and the boys."

Really? He couldn't recall Isi talking about her family. He was always wrapped up in his dating dilemmas and the information had probably gone in one ear and out the other. He swallowed hard. That Isi was all alone in the world didn't seem right. He might have had a mother who cared more about chasing after men, and a father who hadn't wanted the responsibility of raising him, but he'd had siblings and grandparents who cared about him.

"You offered to help," she said. "Would you watch the boys until I find a replacement sitter?"

Babysit? *Him?* "I don't think that's a good idea."

"It would be for two or three days at the most."

"I don't know anything about kids."

She ignored his protests. "I'd need you to drop them off at preschool and bring them back here afterward."

"I'm sure—" he winked at the boys "—they'd rather have anyone but me watch them."

"Never mind." Her shoulders sagged.

Did she have to act so dejected?

"I'll take the boys to school with me and hope the professors allow them into the classroom."

"I don't want to go to your school, Mom," Miguel said.

It's because of me that Isi's nose is broken.

Oh, hell. How hard could it be to watch a couple of four-year-olds? For two years Isi had listened to him bellyache about women. He couldn't turn his back on her when she needed him most.

"Okay, I'll watch the boys," he said.

She flashed him a bright smile. "You'll need to be here by noon on Monday."

"See you then." Right now, Conway couldn't escape fast enough.

Chapter Two

"I don't want a babysitter."

Isi ignored Javier, who sat under the kitchen table playing with his toy cars, and focused on memorizing the Visual Basic code for her exam later in the day.

"How come Conway Twitty Cash has to watch us?" Miguel asked.

Ever since her son had learned Conway's full name, he insisted on using it. For the tenth time, she explained, "Nicole moved to Tucson to live with her father and Mr. Conway is helping us out until I find a new sitter."

Her child-care search had stalled over the weekend. The manager at the preschool had offered Isi the names of three women but none of them had been available to watch the boys at night while she worked at the bar. She worried she'd have to resort to the want ads in the newspaper.

"Mr. Conway's not a girl," Javier said.

"He certainly is not." Conway was all male. Not only did he have a movie-star face, but the way he filled out a pair of jeans turned female heads when he strolled into the bar. Add a boyish grin to his cowboy appeal and every woman on this side of the border was in love with the man.

Too bad he wasn't interested in being a father, because she still experienced an occasional romantic dream about Conway. The day he'd come into the bar and hit on her had been the stuff of fairy tales. Then when he'd learned she was a single mother, he'd cooled toward her. She'd wanted to stay mad at him forever, but he'd continued to visit the bar and joke around with her and in a matter of weeks they'd settled into a cozy friendship. He'd been and always would be her favorite cowboy.

Javier drove a Lego car over the top of her shoe. "Only girls babysit."

"Boys can be sitters, too," she said.

"Conway Twitty Cash, Conway Twitty Cash, Conway Twitty Cash, Con—"

"Enough, Miguel!" Isi shut the textbook. "Names are special and you shouldn't make fun of someone's name."

"Our names are special," Javier said.

She'd named her sons after their twin uncles Javier and Miguel whom they'd never met and never would. Surprisingly, the boys favored their namesakes. Isi's brother Javier had been shy and her brother Miguel had been outgoing—neither had lived long enough to meet their nephews. Isi wished there was a man in her life to help raise the twins, but she'd rather go it alone as a single mom than trust the well-being of her sons to a here-one-day-gone-the-next boyfriend or their biological father, who refused to claim them.

One of the reasons her friendship with Conway had grown was because she enjoyed listening to him talk about his family. When she heard stories about him and his brothers' antics she felt like one of his siblings.

"He's too big for our house," Javier said.

Isi poked her head beneath the table, wincing at the

stab of pain in her nose. "Mr. Conway seems tall because we're all short."

"Do we have to do what Conway Twitty Cash says?" Miguel asked.

"Yes." Isi opened the refrigerator door. "You two wash up while I make lunch." Miguel raced to the bathroom but Javier remained beneath the table. Isi peered at him. "What's the matter?"

"I don't want you to go to school."

"I have an important test this afternoon," she said.

"Are you gonna go to school forever?"

"I hope not." This was her final semester and as long as she passed all her classes, she'd earn an associate degree in business before Christmas. She pulled on her son's shirt until he crawled into the open then she sat him on her lap. "Tell me what's really bothering you, *mi corazón?*" Javier laid his head against her chest. "Mr. Conway's a very nice man," she said. "Did you know he has five brothers and a sister?"

Javier shook his head.

"Maybe when he gets here, you can ask him what it's like to have to share toys with all those brothers." She checked the wall clock. Conway would arrive shortly to drive the boys to preschool—three hours during which she wouldn't have to worry about her sons. It was what went on after Conway picked them up from school that concerned her.

"Everything's going to be okay." She set Javier on his feet and gave him a gentle push in the direction of the bathroom. "Wash your hands."

A half hour later, the boys had eaten their peanut butter and jelly sandwiches and had fetched their backpacks from the bedroom when the doorbell rang.

"It's Conway Twitty Cash!" Miguel raced to the door.

"Use the peephole," Isi said.

Miguel climbed onto the chair next to the door and peered through the spy hole. "It's him." He hopped down and flung open the door. "Hi, Conway Twitty Cash."

Conway grinned. "Hi, Miguel Lopez."

"How come you know I'm Miguel?"

"Because you talk more than your brother." Conway stepped inside. "Hello, Javier."

Javi peeked at Conway from behind Isi's legs. "Thanks for arriving early," she said.

"No problem." His brown-eyed gaze roamed over her body and she resisted glancing at herself to see if she'd spilled food on the front of her blouse.

She motioned to the kitchen table where she'd left a notebook open. "Important numbers are in there. The boys need to be dropped off at school by twelve-thirty and picked up at three-thirty. Supper's between five and six. Bath time is seven. Bedtime eight. I should be home shortly after midnight."

"Where's the school?" Conway asked.

"Over there." Miguel pointed at the kitchen window.

"The Tiny Tot Learn and Play is a mile down the road next to the McDonald's." Isi peeled Javier's arms off her legs, kissed his cheek then gathered her backpack and laptop before kissing Miguel. "Be good for Mr. Conway. If I get a bad report, we won't be going to the carnival this weekend."

She took two steps toward the door before Conway blocked her path. His cologne shot straight up her nose and she sucked in a quick breath. He always smelled nice when he came into the bar. Her eyes narrowed. "What's different about you?"

"I got a haircut," he said.

His shaggy golden-brown hair usually hung over the

collar of his shirt. The shorter style made him appear older, more mature. Less like a playboy. "I like it." His lips curved in his trademark sexy smile. If she didn't leave soon, she'd be tempted to run her fingers through his locks.

He followed her outside. "Don't you want my number in case you need to get in touch with me?"

Duh. She dug her phone from her purse. "What is it?" He recited the digits. "Thanks. My cell number is in the notebook." She turned away then stopped. "I notified the school that you'd be bringing the boys and picking them up for a few days. You'll need to show your license each time. And don't forget to put their booster seats in your truck." She waved at the seats on the porch. "Thanks again!"

Conway watched Isi get into her clunker and drive off then studied his charges. The boys stood side by side, their backpacks strapped on. They wore the same outfit. Jeans, striped T-shirts—Miguel's was red and blue and Javier's was green and blue.

"Aren't we gonna leave, Conway Twitty Cash?" Miguel asked.

"We can't."

The brothers looked at each other, then Miguel asked, "Why not?"

Conway stared at Javier's feet.

Miguel shoved his brother. "You got different shoes on, stupid."

"I know." Javier jutted his chin.

Conway suspected the kid hadn't meant to wear mismatched shoes and was trying to save face. "Cool. I used to wear a different cowboy boot on each foot when I first began rodeoing."

"Why?" Miguel asked.

"For good luck," Conway said. "Is that why you wear different shoes, Javier?"

The boy jiggled his head.

"I wore my good-luck boots all the time and you know what happened?"

"What?" both boys asked.

"They ran out of luck."

Javier raced from the room and returned with matching sneakers.

"Smart man, Javier. Gotta save the good luck for stuff that matters." Crisis averted, Conway ushered the boys out of the trailer and they raced to his truck.

"Hey, does your mom lock the door when she leaves?"

Miguel returned to the porch and plucked a key from the flowerpot of fake daisies on the first step. After Conway secured the trailer, he slipped the key into his pocket and picked up the booster seats. "You guys sit in the front while I figure out how to install these things." Five minutes later, he said, "Okay. Get in them."

The boys climbed in the truck, their shoes dragging across the front seat of the cab as they crawled into their boosters. "Watch the shoes, amigos." Conway's black Dodge was only a year old—he didn't even allow his dates to put their makeup on in his truck. Once the boys were buckled in, he drove off.

There was nowhere to park his big truck in the preschool lot when he arrived, so he pulled into a handicapped spot. He'd no sooner turned off the engine than a woman knocked on the window.

"You can't park here," she said. "You don't have a permit."

"I'm dropping the boys off."

"I'm sorry, but you'll have to use the lot across the street."

"I'll only be a few minutes."

"Doesn't matter." She planted her hands on her hips and he had no doubt that she'd tackle him to the ground if he tried to get out of the truck.

"Hang on, guys." Conway backed out of the spot.

"That's Mrs. Schneider," Miguel said. "We call her Mrs. Spider 'cause she's creepy." The boys giggled.

"She is creepy." Conway parked across the street then helped the boys out of their booster seats. The school bell rang, echoing above the noise from the traffic.

"We get a flag by our name if we're late," Miguel said.

Conway tucked both boys against his sides like footballs and said, "Hold on." Bypassing the crosswalk he dashed across the street then set his cargo on their feet. "Lead the way."

As soon as they entered the building, Miguel marched up to the front desk and said, "This is Conway Twitty Cash."

The day-care employee rolled her eyes. "And I'm Loretta Lynn."

Conway fished his wallet from his pocket. "Isi Lopez called the school and informed someone that I'd be dropping the boys off and picking them up." He set his license on the counter.

The woman read his license. "You're kidding, right?"

"No, ma'am. I'm Conway Twitty Cash."

Miguel grinned at the lady.

"Shouldn't you guys hang up your backpacks?" Conway asked.

The lady handed him a clipboard and pen. "Fill out this form."

He wrote down his full name, cell phone, social security and license numbers plus the color, make and model of his truck. Hell, he was surprised they didn't ask for a credit card. When he finished, he turned away from the desk and plowed into Javier, who'd been standing behind him the whole time.

"Javier doesn't like to come here," the lady whispered then walked off to speak with a parent.

Conway guided the boy to a chair in the waiting area and sat down. "You don't like to come here?"

The kid scuffed his shoe against the floor.

"Are the teachers mean?"

Javier shook his head.

"Are the kids mean?"

He shrugged.

Javier's shyness probably made him an easy target for bullies. Conway peeked into the main room and saw that Miguel sat on the floor with a group of boys. He didn't know what to do. If he left Javier at the school, he'd worry about him being picked on.

"Are you ill?" He touched the boy's forehead. "You feel kind of warm. You think you might be coming down with a cold?"

Javier's eyebrows scrunched together.

"Because if you're getting sick, you shouldn't stay here and infect the other kids."

The boy blinked then he faked a sneeze.

"You are coming down with a cold." Conway spoke with the head of the preschool then waited while she asked Miguel if he wanted to go home with his brother. Miguel elected to remain at school.

Now what? Conway sat in his truck staring at Javier in the rearview mirror. He'd planned to use the time the boys were in school to browse orchard sprayers at a local farm-equipment store. He needed to apply insecticide to the pecan trees before the weevils got out of hand. "You ever been to a tractor store, Javier?" The boy shook his head. "Then it's about time you met John Deere."

Isɪ ᴛᴜʀɴᴇᴅ ɪɴ her exam early and left the classroom. The test had been a breeze—then again she'd studied all weekend. She didn't have the luxury of failing a class or retaking it. She'd qualified for a scholarship to attend the community college and she had to maintain a 3.0 grade point average to keep her financial aid.

She stopped at the school cafeteria for a bite to eat before her next class and while she waited in the sandwich line, she skimmed through phone messages. When she saw the missed call from the preschool, alarm bells went off inside her head. She gave up her place in line and stepped into the hallway to call the school. After learning Conway had signed out Javier because her son hadn't felt well, she dialed Conway's cell. No answer. She left a voicemail, asking him for an update then returned to the cafeteria.

By the time her final class of the day ended, she still hadn't heard from Conway. She contacted the preschool again and they confirmed that Conway and Javier had returned to pick up Miguel. As soon as Isi arrived at the bar, she texted Conway. When he didn't answer, she left another message, pleading with him to get in touch with her. Two hours later, she was about to ask her boss if she could leave work early when Conway strolled into the bar with the twins.

Relieved the three males appeared no worse for wear she delivered a drink order to a table while they claimed seats at the bar. When she approached the group, she felt Javier's forehead. "No fever."

Conway came to her son's defense. "He was warm when we got to the school and I didn't think it was a good idea to leave him there." He ruffled Javier's hair and Isi's heart melted at the affectionate gesture.

"Are you feeling better, Javi?" she asked.

"Yes."

Isi switched her attention to Conway. "Why didn't you return my calls?" This gig wasn't going to work, if they didn't communicate with each other. "I was frantic wondering what was wrong with Javier."

"I'll try to remember to check my phone more often."

She waved a hand in front of her. "What are you doing here?"

"Conway Twitty Cash doesn't cook, Mom." Miguel's gaze swiveled back and forth between Isi and Conway.

Isi got a discount on her meals, but she didn't have the extra money to pay for the boys' food.

As if sensing her dilemma, Conway said, "It's my treat."

Isi guessed it wouldn't hurt for the boys to eat at the bar this one time. She put in an order for three cheeseburger baskets with fries. While she waited tables, she kept an eye on the trio and couldn't help feel a tiny smidgeon of envy that she wasn't sitting with them. Whatever Conway said appeared to amuse her sons, because they giggled an awful lot. Miguel was a talker, so it didn't surprise her that he chatted with Conway. What amazed her was that shy Javier appeared more animated. Maybe Conway's relaxed personality put her son at ease.

That nonchalant attitude would drive Isi nuts after a while. She was a go-getter, get-things-done-do-it-now-not-later kind of woman and Conway came across as a man who went with the flow. Instead of going after the future, he was happy to let the future find him.

A half hour later, the boys had finished eating and were fooling around with the jukebox in the corner.

"That's too much," Isi said when Conway left forty dollars next to the empty food baskets.

"You can never tip enough for great service." He ran his finger along the bridge of her nose. "The swelling's gone down."

"It's not as sore, either." She didn't want to tell him that last night when she'd rolled over in bed and had pressed her face into the pillow, it had felt as if someone had stabbed her up the nose.

"I don't think you'll have a bump."

"I'm not worried about that."

"You should be, because you have a very pretty, petite nose."

She scoffed.

"What?" He leaned closer and whispered. "Just because we're friends, doesn't mean I don't still find you attractive."

Sheesh. The guy was an incurable flirt. The last thing she needed was to allow Conway to slip past her defenses when they both knew they were all wrong for each other. "Javier wasn't really sick, was he?"

"No. And he wouldn't tell me why he didn't want to stay at school."

"There are a couple of boys who tease him, because he's shy. Give him a little encouragement when you drop him off tomorrow."

"You want me to give him a pep talk?"

Conway made her handling of the situation seem stupid.

"Sounds to me like someone needs to tell the bullies to keep their distance from Javier."

"Stay out of this, Conway." The last thing she wanted was her babysitter threatening her sons' classmates. "Red said I could leave early if it's not busy tonight."

He slid off the stool. "How'd your test go?"

Startled by the question, she didn't immediately answer.

"You did have an exam today, didn't you?"

"It went fine. Thanks for asking." She wasn't used to anyone inquiring about her schoolwork.

"See you later." Conway called to the boys and they left the bar.

Isi ignored another sharp twinge of envy when neither of her sons waved goodbye or acted as if they'd missed her. As a matter of fact, they seemed downright gleeful that they were stuck with Conway.

She returned to work, hoping the night would pass quickly. By the time her shift ended and she arrived back at the trailer, she was exhausted and she still had schoolwork to do before going to bed. When she got out of the car and surveyed the mess in the yard, she groaned. Bikes, pogo sticks, footballs, basketballs, baseballs, mitts, bats, scooters and skateboards were strewn about.

Why hadn't Conway demanded the boys put their toys away before turning in for the night? She thought about doing it herself, but she was too tired. When she entered the trailer, the place was dark, save for the light above the kitchen stove. She stood by the door until her eyes adjusted to the dimness.

Conway slept on the love seat, legs hanging over the end, boots off. His sexy sprawl triggered a vision of her coming home to him every night—until he found the perfect woman and left Isi out in the cold.

She padded closer to the couch and studied him. Why had he cut his hair? Had he wanted to impress her? *Dream on.* The shorter hairstyle drew attention to his square jaw and full lips—a mouth made for kissing as she'd discovered a long time ago.

They'd only shared a couple of kisses before Conway had learned she was a single mother, but those kisses had been amazing. The instant their lips had touched, sparks ignited. He'd nibbled her lower lip, making her yearn for more then he'd thrust his tongue inside her mouth and… Isi swallowed a groan and shoved the memory aside.

She glanced at the living room—toys scattered everywhere. When had her sons accumulated so much junk? She'd bought the toys at second-hand stores and rummage sales, but maybe she'd gone overboard. She was the first to admit that she spoiled the twins because she felt guilty for not spending more time with them. Guilty that they didn't have a father. Guilty that they didn't have any family except her.

She retreated to the kitchen, where a sink full of dirty dishes greeted her. The boys must have used a clean cup each time they'd gotten a drink. Next, she went into the bathroom and felt their toothbrushes. Dry as a bone—they'd gone to bed without brushing their teeth. She didn't have dental insurance, so she was strict about making the boys brush and use a daily fluoride rinse. She walked down the hall to their bedroom and poked her head inside. They were sound asleep in their twin beds—fully clothed.

Isi brushed her teeth, changed into her sleeping shorts and T-shirt then slipped into bed, forgetting all about waking Conway and sending him home.

Chapter Three

The rumble of a truck engine woke Isi at the crack of dawn.

Conway! Had he slept on her couch all night long?

She sprang from the bed and raced through the trailer. When she stepped outside, only the taillights of his truck were visible as he turned out of the neighborhood. Her gaze skimmed the yard. Bless Conway's big cowboy heart—he'd put all the toys in the box next to the storage shed and had left the boys' booster seats on the steps. When she went inside to make coffee, she noticed he'd also picked up the living room. Every Lego and building block, toy car, board game and action figure had been stowed in the colored bins against the wall. And in the kitchen, there wasn't a dirty dish in sight.

A lump formed in her throat. She'd thought she known Conway pretty well after their talks at the bar. So how had it escaped her notice, that hiding beneath all that sexy charisma and charm was a considerate man?

Conway's thoughtfulness reminded her of how much she missed her best friend, Erica. Isi had met Erica three years ago at the community college when they'd worked together on a class project. Erica had always been there for Isi, helping her out with the boys when the sitter had become ill. This past spring, Erica had transferred to the University of Southern California to pursue a nursing degree and live closer to her boyfriend.

Feeling weepy, she made coffee and decided to read a chapter for class before the boys woke up. After the twins ate breakfast, she'd resume her search for a sitter.

"You were MIA last night."

Conway stepped away from the tractor where he was in the process of attaching the mist sprayer he'd rented in Yuma the day before. Will hovered in the barn doorway.

The second-eldest Cash brother had once been a tie-down roper, but the past few years he'd spent more time working construction jobs than he did riding the circuit.

"Since when did you start keeping tabs on me?"

"It was Mack's birthday yesterday, you dumb shit."

Well, hell. He'd forgotten. "I was helping a friend out."

Will walked farther into the barn. "I suppose your *friend* needed help with her bed."

His brother's words prompted a vision of Conway slipping between the sheets with Isi. Disturbed at how easily his mind put him and Isi together as a couple he said, "You need to go off and rodeo for a while."

"Why's that?"

"Lately you've been as sociable as a rotting tooth."

"We all can't be as popular with the ladies as you are," Will said.

Normally Conway would relish a game of verbal sparring with his brother, but he didn't have time. "I'll call Mack and wish him a happy birthday." He tested the lock that held the fan sprayer in place then hopped on the tractor seat.

"Where'd you get the sprayer?" Will asked.

"Jim Baine leased it to me."

"Since when did the feed store start renting farm equipment?"

"I don't know, but when I went to Tractor Supply in Yuma to browse sprayers, the salesclerk told me to stop by Jim's, so I did."

"How much did he charge you for it?"

"A hundred dollars for the week." Several months ago their oldest brother Johnny had informed the family that the farm was in financial trouble. Conway and his brothers had pitched in their savings to make up the missed mortgage payments so any new equipment purchases would have to wait.

"I hope you know what you're doing, because I sure as hell would like to get paid back the money I contributed to produce this crop," Will said.

Ever since Johnny had handed over control of the pecan groves to Conway, the rest of his brothers believed it was their duty to comment on how he did things. Will wasn't a farmer, but Conway felt a special connection with the land and he intended to do everything in his power to produce a healthy nut crop and that meant doing things by the book—like spraying for insects during the month of October.

"Don't worry, bro, I've got things under control." Conway grinned. "But if you're willing to help out, you can—"

"No way." Will raised his hands in the air. "I build things. I don't grow them."

"Is the construction business improving?"

"Ben's got several small jobs lined up to keep us busy."

Not busy enough to prevent Will from harassing Conway. "I'd love to chat, but I need to spray a few rows before I leave."

"Where are you going?"

"I'm watching a friend's kids while she goes to school and works at night."

"Your friend wouldn't happen to be a waitress at the Border Town Bar & Grill, would she?" Will asked.

"Why?"

Will chuckled. "You're the guy two women were fighting over when one of them got her nose broken."

"They weren't fighting over me. Isi—"

"Who's Isi?"

"The waitress at the bar. She took a punch that was meant for me."

"Ouch." Will shook his head. "I don't get why women fawn all over you."

"Because I'm the handsome Cash brother." Conway grinned.

"Yeah, right. Wait until word gets around that you're a pecan farmer and not the swaggering rodeo hero you want everyone to believe you are."

Conway didn't give a crap how his new career might affect his image. For a while now he'd been wanting to settle down and it was only a matter of time before he found the right woman.

"This Isi must be special if you're sprucing up for her." Will motioned to Conway's short hair.

Isi was special, but not in the way Will meant. Conway ignored his brother and started the tractor. The engine sputtered and coughed before settling into a loud roar, then he shifted gears and drove out of the barn.

He lined up the sprayer then moved through the first row of trees, contemplating Will's words. There was no reason he couldn't work on the farm and rodeo weekends until he found the woman of his dreams. As a matter of fact, he'd head up to Payson on Saturday and enter the Frontier Days Rodeo. Who knows, maybe he'd run into his soul mate.

"And he let us sit on the tractor," Javier said.

Isi listened to the boys chatter about their day with Conway while she made grilled cheese sandwiches for lunch.

Miguel set two plastic cups on the table. "Next time I get to go."

"And he let me push the brake and—"

"Okay, enough," Isi interrupted Javier, hoping to ward off a fight. Miguel was jealous that his brother had gone to the tractor store with Conway while he'd stayed in preschool.

"I wanna tractor when I grow up," Javier said.

Isi cut the sandwiches in half, placed them on paper plates then added apples slices to the meal. "What would you do with a tractor, Javi?"

"I'd help Mr. Conway on his farm."

"Does Conway Twitty Cash have cows and pigs on his farm?" Miguel asked Isi.

"I don't know, honey." She joined the boys at the table and smoothed the hair off Javier's forehead. "You don't feel warm." He wouldn't make eye contact with her and she reminded herself to tell Conway not to give in to her son if he complained about going to school.

Once the boys ate and brushed their teeth, she sent them outside to play in the yard and began making phone calls. Fifteen minutes later, she'd gotten nowhere—each of the women she'd found in the Sunday want ads had already taken babysitting jobs. Later today she planned to put up a flyer on the campus bulletin board and hoped a student wanting to earn extra cash before Christmas would contact her.

A knock rattled the door. "It's me." Conway stepped into the trailer and his smile faltered. "You're upset. What's wrong?"

For a man who spent yesterday chasing after two demanding four-year-olds and sleeping on a dollhouse-size couch, he looked well-rested.

Well-rested? That was a unique way to describe *sexy*.

Isi ignored the voice in her head. "I'm not upset. I'm discouraged." She closed her notebook. "I haven't had any luck finding a sitter."

"Did you try the online classifieds?" He stopped next to the table and his half smile tugged a sigh from Isi.

"I don't trust those online sites," she said.

"Why not?"

"They're full of child predators." Poor Conway. He was really clueless about raising children.

"Can you put them in day care after school?" he asked.

"There isn't a facility open until midnight." She waved a hand in the air. "Besides, I don't have the money for extended child care."

"I suppose I could keep watching the boys until you find a new sitter."

"You can't be serious."

"Why not?"

She laughed. "The twins are a lot of work."

"They aren't so bad."

Wait until he spent more time with her sons, then the novelty would wear off. She went to the window to make sure the boys were in the yard. "I told Javier that he has to stay at school. Please don't let him talk you into signing him out."

"I wanted to speak to you about that."

She stuffed her books into her backpack.

"Javier told me that he's getting picked on at recess."

"You mean teased?" she said.

"Why haven't you spoken to his teacher about it?"

Isi jerked as if he'd slapped her. "You think I've ignored the problem?"

He shrugged. "Then why are the brats still tormenting Javier?"

Angry that Conway believed she was an uncaring mother, she lashed out. "I don't know what he told you, but his teacher assured me the situation is being dealt with." An image of her son cornered by miniature thugs on the playground popped into Isi's mind. She felt bad that the boys had been placed in day cares and preschools the past three years, but she'd had no choice—not if she intended to make a better life for them. Isi blinked hard.

"You're not going to cry, are you?"

"No." She fussed with her backpack.

Conway wiped the pad of his thumb across her cheekbone, catching the tear that escaped her eye. "I didn't mean to upset you."

She sniffed. "It's… I don't have… Never mind."

"Never mind what? Talk to me."

"I'm doing the best I can, Conway. I complained to the head of the preschool that Javier said kids were picking on him, but she insisted that the boys would work things out on their own."

"How long ago did you speak to this lady?"

"I guess it's been a month."

Conway's jaw hardened. "I can help. Will you trust me to handle this?"

"You don't have any experience with kids."

"I grew up fighting bullies who picked on me because of my name."

His comment triggered more tears. "The teacher said I should encourage the boys' father to become more involved in their lives, but that'll never happen."

"Why?"

"Their father refuses to acknowledge that the boys are his."

Conway scowled. "Make him take a paternity test."

"He's already married with kids."

"You slept with a married man?" Conway gaped at her.

"He didn't tell me he was married."

"And you didn't ask him?"

"He wasn't wearing a wedding band, so I assumed he was single."

"The boys' father should be paying child support. If he helped out financially, you could afford day care." Conway swept his hand in front of him. "You're barely getting by raising them on your own."

"We're fine." She wasn't proud of accepting government assistance to help meet her monthly expenses and put food on the table, but as soon as she earned her degree, she'd find a full-time job with benefits and be able to support herself and the boys all on her own.

"Being a single parent isn't easy." She swallowed hard. "I have no one to—"

Conway cut her off midsentence by pressing his finger against her lips. The tip of his finger slipped past her lip and touched her tongue. A spark of heat warmed her brown eyes as they locked gazes.

"What are you doing?" she mumbled against his finger.

"Trying to stop you from talking."

Did he have any idea how long it had been since a man had touched her so intimately? Feeling short of breath, she said, "Don't do that again."

Good grief. No sense playing with fire when they were both destined for different futures—Conway wanted marriage without kids and if she ever committed to a man, he would have to love her boys as much as she loved them.

"Is my touch that awful?" His eyes sparkled with humor.

"Stop trying to distract me."

"Isi. You're a great mom and the boys are lucky to have you in their corner. Let me help Javier."

Just because you accept his help doesn't mean you're a failure. "Fine." She slung her backpack over her shoulder. "See you after midnight."

Isi stepped outside and blew kisses to the boys. "Be good." Then she drove off, thinking she'd better keep her guard up around Conway in case he turned out to be an authentic Mr. Nice Guy—a Mr. Nice Guy who rocked her world. Again.

WHEN CONWAY ENTERED the preschool, he strode up to the desk and announced, "I'm staying with the boys."

Both Miguel and Javier smiled.

"You can't stay," the lady said.

Conway peered at her name tag. "Why not, Rose? I'd like to observe what the boys do during their time here."

"I can tell you what they do. First, they sit in a circle for story time then—"

"I don't want to hear about it, I want to experience it." Conway tapped his finger against the sign-in sheet on the clipboard. "Is there a guest form I need to fill out?"

Flustered, Rose said, "Wait here, Mr. Cash. I'll get the director."

Miguel tugged on Conway's pant leg. "Now you're in trouble. Ms. Kibble's mean."

"You guys go hang up your backpacks. I'll be there in a minute."

After the boys walked away, an older woman with a salt-and-pepper bob stepped from her office. "Mr. Cash, I understand you'd like to observe today."

"Yes, ma'am." He held out his hand.

"Is there a problem with Miguel or Javier?" she asked.

"Well, ma'am, there is. It seems Javier is being picked on and nothing's been done to address the problem."

The director's eyes rounded and Rose made a hasty exit.

"This is the first I've heard of any bullying going on in my school," Ms. Kibble said.

"No, ma'am, it's not. According to the boys' mother, she's spoken to you about this before, and because the teasing hasn't stopped, Javier doesn't want to come to school anymore."

"Which boys are bothering him?"

"He won't say, but I intend to find out."

"I appreciate your concern, Mr. Cash. I'll make sure the teacher is aware of the situation."

"Good. I'm eager to see how she deals with the bullies."

Ms. Kibble's mouth tightened, but she backed down. "Enjoy your afternoon."

When Conway joined the boys for story time on the floor, Miguel whispered to the kid next to him, "That's Conway Twitty Cash. He's my new friend."

Javier inched closer to Conway but remained silent.

Story time turned out to be boring as hell and it was all Conway could do to keep his eyes open. When the teacher—Ms. Haney—closed the book and asked if anyone had questions, Conway raised his hand.

"Yes, Mr. Cash?"

"When's recess?" The room erupted in giggles, which earned Conway a dark scowl from the teacher.

"Go to your tables and start your work sheets," the teacher said.

When the kids bolted in all directions, a boy walked past Javier and elbowed him in the back. Conway noticed the teacher's attention was elsewhere. The boy with the sharp elbow sat at the same table as Javier, and Javier refused to make eye contact with the kid.

One bully identified. Now he needed to find the others. The only way to do that was to sit away from Javier. He joined Miguel at his table and Conway's gut twisted at Javier's hurt expression. It was all he could do not to rush to the boy's side and reassure him.

While the group worked on their alphabet sheets, Conway watched Javier. Nothing out of the ordinary happened until the teacher asked the students to pass the papers to the head of the table. A freckled-faced boy swept Javier's paper onto the floor then stepped on it before putting it back in the pile and handing it to the teacher.

Bully number two identified.

The class spent the next hour moving from activity to activity until snack time. Fruit punch, crackers and small boxes of raisins were doled out to each kid. Miguel stuffed his face, eating everything in front of him and asking for seconds of the punch. Javier didn't touch his food—or rather he didn't have a chance to, because the red-haired bully had stolen his box of raisins and Javier hadn't protested.

By the time recess arrived, Conway was spitting mad that the teacher hadn't noticed what was happening right under her nose. He followed the kids outside and Javier raced to the swings while Miguel veered off toward the monkey bars and a group of gossiping girls.

When the bullies closed in on Javier, Conway made his move. "Mind if I join you guys on the swings?"

The freckle-faced boy crossed his arms over his chest. "We were playing here first."

Insolent bugger.

"Yeah." The chubby kid kicked dirt at Javier. "He's on our swing."

"This is your swing? You brought this from home?" Conway asked.

Javier giggled then sobered quickly when the bullies glared at him.

"I think you guys have got it wrong. This swing belongs to the school."

"Get off, stupid," the redhead told Javier.

Javier made a move to vacate his seat, but Conway set his hand on his shoulder. "You'll have to wait your turn, carrottop."

"Says who?" the kid glared.

"Says me, Rico." Javier stood and faced his adversary.

Rico laughed. "You can't stop me."

"Yes, I can." Javier shoved Rico in the chest and the kid tripped over his feet and stumbled. Once he gained his balance, Rico swung his fist, but Javier ducked and tackled the boy to the ground. Conway sent the overweight bully a stay-where-you-are glare while Javier and Rico wrestled.

Tiny fists punched mostly air, then a student alerted the playground monitor and the woman hurried over and separated the boys. Holding each by the back of the shirt collar she spoke to Conway. "You stood there and did nothing."

"The boys had to settle this between themselves," Conway said.

"Well, I've never heard of—"

"Lady, if you'd have been doing your job rather than texting on your phone, you'd know that Rico and his buddy like to torment kids."

The woman marched the boys into the building and Conway followed at a distance. Twice Javier peeked over his shoulder and grinned at him. Now that Rico and the other kid knew Javier could stand up for himself, they'd leave him alone.

Conway stood outside Ms. Kibble's office while the playground monitor explained the situation. All three boys were suspended for fighting and told not to return to school until Friday. Grinning from ear to ear, Javier followed Conway out of the school.

"Is my mom gonna be mad at me?" Javier asked.

"Nah." *She's going to be mad as hell at me.*

CONWAY HEARD ISI'S car pull beneath the carport and he braced himself. When the trailer door opened, he said, "I can explain, Isi."

"Explain what?" She flashed a nervous smile.

"Didn't the school call you?"

The blood drained from her face. "What happened? Are the boys okay?"

"They're fine." He hadn't meant to scare her.

She set her backpack by the door. "What's going on?"

He didn't think this would be hard but the speech

he'd rehearsed after the boys had gone to bed suddenly didn't sound so clever. "Javier's been expelled from school until Friday."

Isi's eyes widened. "What happened?"

"It wasn't his fault. You can blame me."

"What did he do, Conway?"

"He got into a fight on the playground."

She gasped.

"None of the boys were hurt. I watched the whole thing and—"

"You watched the fight and didn't break it up?"

"Let me explain." He shoved a hand through his hair. "I stayed at school and monitored their class. As I suspected, Javier is being bullied by two boys, one named Rico and the other one was a chubby kid."

"Mathew."

"During recess Javier got to the swings first but the bullies tried to make him get off. I told the boys Javier didn't have to give up his swing and all of a sudden Javi shoved Rico. The boys rolled on the ground until the recess monitor intervened and took them to the principal's office."

"Was Javier upset?"

"Nope."

"What did Ms. Kibble say?"

"Not a whole lot."

"Were all the boys suspended?"

"Yep. You'd have been proud of Javier, Isi."

"I'm supposed to be happy that you taught my son to solve his problems by fighting?"

"I didn't teach him to fight. I taught him to stand up for himself."

"Do me a favor and don't offer my sons any advice, okay? I'm their mother. I'll handle their problems." Isi walked down the hall to check on the twins and Conway made a hasty escape before he got suspended from his babysitting job.

Chapter Four

When Conway stepped inside Isi's trailer Friday at noon, he came face-to-face with two pouting grumps.

"What's wrong?"

"I found a sitter," Isi said.

A weird feeling gripped Conway's stomach, but he blamed it on the three breakfast burritos he'd eaten earlier in the morning. "Is it—" he motioned to the boys "—because of the school suspension?"

"Not at all," she said. He noticed she didn't make eye contact with him. "A customer at the bar recommended her aunt."

The swelling in Isi's nose had gone down and the bruising beneath her eyes had faded to a yellow hue. If she wore makeup, no one would be able to tell she'd broken her nose. His gaze drifted to her shirt—she looked hot in the black tank top that hugged her small breasts and the threadbare jeans that made her short legs appear a lot longer than they were. He imagined sliding the strap of the shirt off her shoulder and caressing the exposed skin with his tongue, then licking a trail up her neck toward her ear....

Whoa. Hold on, cowboy. What the heck was wrong with him? When had his brain decided to travel south and vacation in his crotch?

Since you started watching the twins.

Isi was an attractive woman and it wouldn't take much effort on her part to jumpstart his libido, especially because he wasn't dating other women. As of right now, Isi was the only female taking up space in his thoughts.

"The new sitter's name is Maria," Isi said. "She'll take the boys to school and pick them up and stay until bedtime. Then my neighbor Mrs. Sneed will come over and watch TV until I get home from work." Isi handed him a sheet of paper.

Conway caught her scent. The combination of flowery perfume and warm female sent a blast of testosterone through his bloodstream. He focused on the note. Isi had written down Maria's full name, address, birth date and a bunch of numbers—driver's license, social security and cell phone.

"What's this for?" he asked.

"I need you to take Maria to the school and show her the ropes." Isi took a deep breath. "She doesn't speak English very well and Rose is the only employee at the school who's bilingual. If she's not working, please give Maria's information to whoever's at the front desk."

"How am I supposed to show Maria anything, if I can't communicate with her?"

"Javier and Miguel will interpret for you."

"I didn't know they spoke Spanish," Conway said.

"They're not fluent, but they should be able to understand most of what Maria says." Isi slung the backpack over her shoulder. "I have to meet with my academic advisor before class, otherwise I'd stay and introduce you to Maria."

"Are you sure this is a good idea?" What if he and Maria got their messages mixed up?

"Stop worrying. Everything will be fine." Isi opened the door. "Thanks for helping with the boys this week."

"No problem."

She paused on the porch. "I'll probably see you at the bar."

"Yeah, I'll drop by." As he watched Isi's sashaying fanny walk to her car, he worried that their relationship would never be the same as it was before he'd offered to watch her sons. Once she drove off, he said, "Are you guys going to be grouchy all day?"

"We don't want Maria," Miguel said.

"I bet she can cook." His comment drew no response.

After the short amount of time he'd spent with the twins, it was nice to know they'd miss him. "You gotta give Maria a chance. I can't watch you guys forever."

"Why not?" Javier asked.

"The pecan harvest starts next month in November. There's a lot I need to do on the farm to get ready for it."

"We could help." Miguel tugged his brother by the shirtsleeve and dragged him across the room until they stood in front of Conway. "We can pick nuts."

"I appreciate the offer, but you guys have to stay in school."

"How come?" Javier asked.

"Because that's what kids do. They go to school to get smart and then they go to college like you're mom is doing."

"Did you go to college?" Miguel asked.

"Nope."

"How come?"

"Do you always ask a lot of questions?"

Both boys bobbed their heads.

"I didn't go to college because I didn't have anyone telling me I should. Then I got older and figured out that what I wanted to do with my life didn't require a college degree."

"What did you want to do?" Miguel asked.

"I wanted to be a pecan farmer."

Javier's nose wrinkled. "I thought you were a cowboy."

"I'm a cowboy when I rodeo on the weekends."

"Can we rodeo?" Miguel asked.

Conway wasn't about to let the munchkins change the subject. "I bet Maria's a nice lady."

"What if she's mean?" Javier's brown eyes pleaded with Conway.

"Then we'll tell your mom." And let Isi deal with the situation. From now on he'd keep his advice to himself.

The sound of a vehicle pulling up to the trailer drifted through the screen door. "That's Maria. You guys be on your best behavior." Conway stepped onto the porch.

Holy moly. The woman was as old and gnarled as the root of an ancient oak tree. She had more wrinkles than a ten-year-old road map. Polyester slacks, a silk-printed long-sleeve blouse with a navy blazer and low-heeled shoes was hardly proper attire for chasing after boys. Then again, this woman was so old, if she chased anything, she'd drop dead of a heart attack.

"*Hola,* Maria." *Hola* and *sí* were about the only words Conway knew in Spanish.

She smiled, the gesture generating more facial wrinkles. He motioned for her to follow him inside. "Miguel, ask Maria what she'd like you to call her?"

Miguel translated Conway's words then Maria spoke.

"What did she say?" Conway asked.

"She said we can call her La Anciana."

Javier giggled.

"Okay." Conway pointed at Maria and smiled. "La

Anciana." Then he indicated himself and said, "Conway" before moving his finger to the kitchen wall clock. "Miguel, tell La Anciana that it's time to leave for school and she should follow us in her car."

After Miguel spoke, Conway waited for the boys to get their backpacks then he held the door open for everyone. When Maria walked by him, her mouth curled in a snarl and he couldn't figure out what the heck he'd done to tick her off.

When they arrived at the school, Rose wasn't working. Conway turned over Maria's information to the lady at the counter and explained that the boys' new sitter didn't speak English and that she'd be dropping the boys off and picking them up after school.

While the employee filled out Maria's paperwork, Conway spoke to the boys. "Miguel, play with your brother at recess." This was Javier's first day back after his suspension. "And no fighting, Javi." Conway hoped Miguel would stick by his brother's side and ward off any threats by the bullies.

"Are you gonna pick us up?" Miguel asked.

"Yes. Tell Maria that she's to meet me back here at three-thirty." He wanted to make sure she didn't forget to return for the boys.

Miguel translated and Maria responded.

"What did she say?" Conway asked.

"She wants to know if she's supposed to wash our clothes."

Conway was certain Isi would appreciate help with the housework. "Sure. Tell her she can wash clothes if she wants."

Miguel translated then said, "She wants to know what you're going to do."

"I'll be at the farm."

After Miguel conveyed the information, Conway said, "Have fun." He tipped his hat to Maria then left the building.

Anxiety gnawed at his gut as he drove away from the school. Isi was desperate to find a sitter for the boys, but Maria wasn't the right fit. The twins needed a young energetic person who would play outside with them. By the time he reached the edge of town, he'd broken out in a cold sweat. Instead of heading to the farm, he made a U-turn. He'd feel better if he stayed close by in case Javier got into trouble again at school.

A SIXTH SENSE told Isi she needed to go home after her classes and see how Maria and the boys were getting along, so she'd called in sick to work. She hoped the day had gone well and her sons had been on their best behavior, but she couldn't ignore a nagging suspicion that not all was right. When she'd interviewed Maria over the phone, the woman hadn't sounded very peppy but after raising five children of her own, she was certainly experienced enough to handle the twins. Even so, Isi worried the boys would be too taxing on the seventy-year-old woman.

She turned into the mobile home park and saw Conway's truck next to the trailer. *Uh-oh.* She parked beneath the carport and got out of the car. Conway was throwing the football with Miguel and Javier played with a Slinky on the porch steps.

"Watch this, Mom." Miguel tossed the ball to Conway.

"Where's Maria?" she asked.

"She left," Conway said.

"She was supposed to stay with the boys until Mrs. Sneed came over at eight o'clock."

"I don't know what happened," Conway said. "Everything was going fine until she took her purse and stormed out of the trailer."

"I thought you'd planned to work on the farm after you dropped the boys off at school," Isi said.

"I had errands to do in town."

Something smelled fishy. Isi noticed that Javier wouldn't make eye contact with her. "Miguel, what happened?"

He shrugged.

"Come to think of it," Conway said, "Maria seemed agitated when we called her La Anciana, but—"

Isi gasped.

"What?" Conway's gaze bounced between her and Miguel.

"You called her La Anciana?"

"That's what Miguel said she wanted us to call her."

"You insulted her. *La Anciana* means old lady. It's a derogatory term." Isi glared at her sons. "We'll discuss this later."

"I thought you were working at the bar tonight," Conway said.

"I called in sick, because I had a funny feeling about today. Good thing I listened to my instincts."

"I'm sorry. I didn't mean to insult Maria," Conway said. "I'd be happy to apologize to her."

Isi appreciated his offer, but waved it off. "What else happened?"

"Maria asked if she should wash clothes while the boys were in school and I said sure, thinking you'd appreciate the help. When we got home from school she had all the laundry done."

Dear Lord, there had been at least six loads of clothes piled on the laundry room floor.

"And I told her to clean our bedrooms and do the dishes," Miguel said.

"Cleaning the bedroom is your responsibility, Miguel." Isi rubbed her aching forehead. "What else did you tell Maria to do?"

"Nothing."

Javier tattled on his brother. "He dumped all the toys out of the bins after Maria picked them up."

Isi thought she'd hired a woman experienced enough to stand up to her sons and not let them run roughshod over her. "Is Maria coming back on Monday?"

Miguel played with the laces on his sneakers.

"She's coming back, right?" Conway nudged Miguel's shoulder.

Her son shook his head.

"Why isn't she coming back?" Isi asked.

"'Cause I told her not to." Miguel stamped his foot. "We want Conway to take care of us."

"You two go inside and wash up for supper while I speak with Conway," she said.

Miguel glared at her and she was tempted to paddle his bottom for being disrespectful.

Once the trailer door closed and the boys were out of earshot, Conway spoke. "I had no idea what Miguel was saying to Maria. Had I known he was being rude and misleading her, I would have stopped him."

"I shouldn't have put you in this position." She felt bad for Maria and bad for Conway, both having been duped by a pair of four-year-olds. "I'll call Maria later and apologize. Hopefully, she'll agree to return on Monday."

"What if she doesn't?"

"Then I'll ask Mrs. Sneed to fill in until I find a sitter."

"Will she watch the boys for free?"

"Probably not. I'll have to scratch a few items off the boys' Christmas lists to come up with the money to pay her." Isi abruptly shut her mouth. Since when did she unload her problems on Conway? She was the advice-giver not the advice-seeker.

"I'll tell you what," he said. "I'll watch the boys until you graduate at the end of the semester." Then he added. "For free. It'll be my graduation gift to you."

For a man dead set against fatherhood, it was a generous offer. "You're busy with the farm, and what about your rodeos?"

"I'll manage. Well, there might be a problem unless..."

"Unless what?"

"You allow the boys to miss a few days of school the middle of November when I harvest the pecans."

"The boys will get in your way."

"I'll put them to work. Once I drive the shaker machine through a row of trees, they can collect the twigs and sticks that fall to the ground. And we've got extra beds in the bunkhouse they can sleep in."

"I don't know, Conway. They could be more of a hindrance than a help. I have to nag them to do their chores."

"Farming isn't sissy work like making beds or washing dishes."

"Sissy work?" Isi struggled not to laugh. "There's nothing wrong with a man who picks up after himself and keeps a clean house."

"You were the one who said their teacher suggested you ask the boys' father to become involved in their lives. I'm not their father, but I'm offering the boys a chance to do guy stuff."

She shook her head.

"What?"

"I can't believe what I'm hearing." When he frowned, she said, "I've spent the past two years listening to you insist you don't want kids and now you're offering to watch mine 24/7."

Conway flashed a grin and her breath caught in the back of her throat. All the man had to do was smile to get his way. "What happens if the boys decide they don't want to stay at the farm all day and night?"

"Then you threaten to bring Maria back."

"That might work." It would be a weight off of her shoulders not having to worry about child care while she studied for finals and worked on her research paper. "Okay, but I'll pay you."

He chuckled. "I've used you for my personal therapist the past two years."

"You consider me your therapist?"

His gaze roamed over her body, and a delicious heat spread through her belly. "Yes, ma'am, I do." He winked. "And I'm sure I'll need more therapy, if I'm to survive the next two months with Mig and Javi."

"I'll think about it, Conway, but until I make up my mind, please don't say anything to the boys."

"Tomorrow's Saturday," he said. "Do you have to work at the bar?"

"No, I'm taking the boys to the carnival."

"What carnival?"

"Every year a small carnival sets up in the Walmart parking lot. It's only a few rides, games and lots of junk-food vendors." It was cheap entertainment.

"Can Conway go with us?" Miguel asked, smashing his face against the screen.

"Conway has better things to do than ride the Ferris wheel and eat cotton candy. And stop eavesdropping, Miguel."

"Do you like cotton candy, Conway?" Javier asked.

"Sure do."

It hadn't escaped Isi's notice that Javi had opened up to Conway this week. If anyone had told her that this man, who never wanted to be a father, would be great with kids, she would have thought they had a screw loose.

"What time are you leaving for the carnival?" he asked.

"I'd like to get there when it opens at ten." As the day wore on the boys would become cranky.

Conway dug his keys from his pocket and walked to his truck. "I'll pick you up at nine forty-five."

Isi hurried after him. "You don't have to do this," she said. "They'll understand if I tell them you're busy."

He opened the truck door. "Isi?"

"What?"

"I'm not doing this for the boys."

"You aren't?"

He shook his head. "I'm doing it for me."

"You've been dying to go to a carnival?"

"No." He slid on his sunglasses then flashed a devil-may-care smile. "But it beats the heck out of getting bucked off a bull."

As soon as Conway drove off, Javier's "I'm hungry" snapped Isi out of her trance.

"Hey, Dixie." Conway climbed the farmhouse steps early Saturday morning and quietly walked to the end of the porch where his sister, the baby of the Cash clan, sat on the swing with her three-month-old son, Nathan.

He leaned against the rail and whispered, "How's the little guy doing?"

"He finally fell asleep."

Nate had been colicky since birth, but Dixie's husband, Gavin, had the patience of a saint and walked the floors with the baby. Keeping his voice low, he asked, "Has he been up all night?"

"Yes. I took over walking him an hour ago so Gavin could sleep."

Conway peered at the fuzzy dark head. "I can't believe he's got all that hair."

His sister released a deep sigh.

"What's wrong?"

"I never thought I'd say this, Conway, but I'm ready to buy a house in Yuma. Commuting to the gift shop every day with the baby is too exhausting."

"But you love this place." Their grandmother had willed the farmhouse to Dixie, trusting her granddaughter to keep it in the family.

"After Nate was born I realized it's the memories of growing up here that I love most. The house is only walls and doorways and light switches. It's what went on in each of the rooms that will stay with me the rest of my life."

"Is Gavin pushing you to move to Yuma?" Conway's brother-in-law worked for the city on water reclamation projects and spent most of his day in his truck driving to various sites.

"Not at all. But it seems like the only time Gavin sees Nate is in the middle of the night when he's crying. And maybe if Nate didn't have to spend so much time in the car, he might sleep better."

"What do you want to do with the house? Rent or sell?"

"Neither."

Conway gaped at his sister. "You made us all move out because you and Gavin wanted privacy. Now it's going to sit empty?"

"I thought maybe Johnny and Shannon might want the house."

"Johnny works at the Triple D. It wouldn't make sense for them to drive back to the ranch every day when Johnny's out of bed at the crack of dawn feeding cattle."

"Okay, then whichever of my brothers marries next can lay claim to the house."

"The place will sit empty forever."

"Considering how picky *you* are when it comes to women, you'll never get the chance to live in this house."

"What do you mean picky?"

"Women swoon when you walk by them." Dixie smiled. "But you find fault with every female you date."

It wasn't that he found anything wrong with his dates, it was that the ladies weren't always truthful with him when they claimed to be on board with his no-kids itinerary. The women who'd said they didn't want kids tried to change Conway's mind after they'd gone out on several dates.

"I'm picky," he said. "So what?"

"Does your father have anything to do with you not wanting kids?"

Dixie was too perceptive for her own good.

"Have you ever been in contact with your dad?" she asked.

"Nah." He dropped his gaze so she wouldn't catch him in a lie.

No one in the family knew that when Conway turned eighteen, he'd tracked down Zachary Johnson—the man who'd gotten his mother pregnant but had refused to marry her. Since Conway and his brothers had been fathered by different men, their mother had put her surname on all their birth certificates, but she'd listed Zachary Johnson as Conway's father. Conway found the man working as a ranch hand on a spread in northern Arizona. To his surprise the man hadn't been upset that Conway had found him. When asked why he'd walked out on Conway and his mother, his father said he hadn't known how to stay. Zachary Johnson's father and grandfather before him had all walked out on the women they'd gotten pregnant.

From that day forward he'd decided he wouldn't be like his father or grandfather and abandon his children. The only way he could guarantee breaking that cycle was marrying a woman who didn't want kids.

"Now that I have Nathan, I think it would be nice if he had a grandfather."

"Nate's got plenty of uncles." An image of Miguel and Javier flashed before Conway's eyes and he felt bad for the boys that their father wasn't involved in their lives. The twins were still young, but it wouldn't be long before they asked Isi why their father wanted nothing to do with them. Conway had been seven the first time he'd asked his mom that same question.

Nate began fussing and Conway held out his arms. "Give to him to me."

The baby was the size of a football. "He's getting fat—you're feeding him too much."

"Since when are you an expert on babies?"

"Hey, I can be objective, because I don't intend to have kids."

"You'd make a great father."

He shook his head. "When I marry, I plan to spend

all my free time with my wife." That's what he told everyone whenever the subject of marriage and kids came up. Better to have others believe he was selfish rather than admit he was afraid if he had kids he'd leave them high and dry for no good reason other than an inherited genetic instinct to flee.

"You'd feel differently if you had your own child," Dixie said.

"I'm sure Nate will have plenty of cousins to play with in time."

"You'd better get going if you want to catch up with Porter. He left for the rodeo a half hour ago."

"I'm not going to the rodeo."

"Why not?"

"I'm not telling." He kissed the top of Nate's fuzzy head. "He smells good on top, but his bottom stinks." He handed his nephew back to Dixie.

She sniffed his diaper and made a face.

"I won't have to worry." He skipped down the steps.

"Worry about what?" Dixie called after him.

"My house smelling like baby vomit and dirty diapers."

As he drove away from the farm, he reminded himself to stop at the bank once he got to Yuma. He sure hoped the pecan harvest was abundant this year—making amends for Isi's broken nose was costing him a fortune.

Chapter Five

Conway stood in the middle of the Walmart parking lot holding the twins' hands as they gazed up at the Ferris wheel while Isi waited in line to buy tickets for the ride.

"Have you ever been on a Ferris wheel?" he asked the boys.

Javier nodded, then Miguel said, "Our mom loves the Ferris wheel."

As Conway watched the huge wheel rotate, its occupants waving to friends and family on the ground, he struggled to understand how he'd reached the age of twenty-eight and had yet to visit a Six Flags amusement park, SeaWorld, Disneyland or a circus.

He didn't often allow his thoughts to drift back to his early childhood, because of memories he'd just as soon forget—a mother who'd been in and out of his life and a father who'd gone AWOL six months after his birth. His grandparents did their best to love seven grandchildren, but caring for their daughter's brood had worn them out and stretched their finances to the limit—there had never been extra money to take the family to a carnival.

Javier squeezed Conway's hand. "Are you afraid?"

"I don't know. I've never been on a Ferris wheel."

"We got a deal on the tickets," Isi said when she joined them.

"What kind of deal?" he asked.

"Early-bird special—two-for-one." She smiled. "That means there's an extra ride in the budget."

"Conway's never been on a Ferris wheel, Mom," Miguel said.

"Really?" Isi leaned in and whispered in Conway's ear. "Are you afraid of heights?"

"I don't know. Guess I'll find out," he said.

Isi smiled. "I'll hold your hand."

"Me, too," Javier said.

After the riders got off, the carnival worker ushered the four of them into one seat, the boys squeezing between Isi and Conway. When the seat lurched forward, Conway clutched the safety bar across their laps. As they made their way to the top of the wheel, he decided he definitely didn't like heights. Instead of staring at the ground he focused on Isi. He reached behind the boys' heads and ran his finger lightly down her dainty nose. "No bump."

"I was wondering when the swelling went down if I'd be left with a hockey player's snout," she said.

Isi was a pretty girl—any guy would be lucky to have her and the twins.

As long as it's not you.

Startled by the voice in his head, he pulled his arm back and glanced down too quickly. His head spun and he closed his eyes.

The pressure of a tiny hand on his thigh forced his eyes open. Javier's brow scrunched with worry and Conway grasped his fingers. Javier smiled, the gesture tweaking Conway's heart. He pulled in a deep breath and stared straight ahead, spotting a hot air balloon in the distance. "Check that out, guys." He pointed to the west.

"Can we ride in one of those, Mom?" Miguel asked.

"No, honey," Isi said.

Miguel leaned in front of his brother. "Will you ride in a balloon with me, Conway?"

"Conway's busy with his farm, Miguel," Isi said before he could answer the boy.

After one more rotation, the ride ended. "What's next?" Conway asked.

Javier motioned to a game booth where a girl held a giant stuffed polar bear. "Win us one of those, Conway."

"Yeah—" Miguel chimed in "—win us a bear."

Nothing like pressure. "Let's go see." Conway had been the second-string pitcher on his high-school baseball team—he ought to be able to knock over a few milk bottles.

"Five balls for five dollars! Everyone wins a prize!" The carnival worker shouted at the passing crowd.

"I might need a few warm-up throws," Conway said. Ten dollars later, he still hadn't thrown a strike.

"That's okay, we don't need a bear." Javier was letting Conway off the hook and that made him feel worse.

"You can do it." Miguel didn't want Conway to give up.

"Boys, we've spent enough money. Let's find a new game." Isi attempted to steer the twins away from the booth.

Miguel wouldn't be deterred. "Wait, Mom. Conway can do it."

The boys had too much faith in him and he didn't want to disappoint them. "I'll give it one more try." He handed the carnival worker a ten-dollar bill and ignored the soreness in his elbow as he wound up for the throw.

No luck. When the booth attendant handed Conway

his last ball, he whispered, "Don't throw so hard and hit the pin left of the center."

Conway threw the ball and the milk bottles tumbled like dominos.

"You did it, Conway!" Miguel jumped up and down and Javier clapped his hands.

He high-fived the boys, relieved he hadn't made a fool of himself in front of Isi.

Since when have you ever cared what Isi thinks of you?

Since he didn't know when—he just did.

The game attendant handed the boys the huge polar bear, which had ended up costing Conway forty dollars. "I'll take the bear to the truck." He handed Isi a twenty. "Buy the boys some cotton candy and I'll catch up with you."

"Meet us at the Scrambler," she said.

Later when Conway arrived at the ride, Isi said, "Perfect timing." Their turn came, but she blocked Miguel from boarding first. "Let Conway sit on the end, then me, then you two."

"You don't want them to sit between us?" Conway asked.

"The person who boards first gets smashed the worst during this ride."

With Isi pressed tightly against his side, it was impossible not to breathe in the scent of her perfume. Conway broke out in a sweat that had nothing to do with the sun beating down on his head.

The ride began, building momentum, pushing Isi's body into his. He swore the friction between their limbs was going to set their clothes on fire. Her laughter rang out along with the boys, but Conway didn't find anything funny about the feel of Isi's breast rubbing his arm.

When the ride slowed down, her gaze connected with his. He'd lost himself in Isi's eyes before but had never felt short of breath like he did now.

When the ride came to a complete stop, the attendant released the safety latch on the seat and they piled out. As they walked away, Conway heard someone call his name and he stopped. An attractive blonde waved a balloon in the air. *Sara*... He couldn't recall her last name. Sara approached with a child in tow and Conway felt Isi stiffen next to him.

"Long time no see, Conway."

"Sara, this is Isi and her sons Javier and Miguel. Isi, this is Sara…"

"Reynolds." Sara stroked the girl's hair. "My niece, Tiffany."

"Nice to meet you," Isi said, noticing Sara's perplexed expression.

"I never expected to run into you at a kids' carnival," Sara said.

The lightbulb finally went off inside Isi's head. Sara had been the woman Conway had dated this past February. He'd told Isi that he believed she'd been *the one* but like all the other women he'd pursued, Sara hadn't been truthful in the beginning with him about wanting children. It wasn't until they'd been together almost a month that she'd admitted she'd like a baby one day.

There was no mistaking the predatory gleam in Sara's eye—obviously she believed Conway had changed his mind about children. Isi might as well set the woman straight. "Conway, take the boys to get a hot dog. I'll catch up in a minute."

Isi told herself she was looking out for Conway's best

interests and warning Sara away from him had nothing to do with her own growing feelings for the cowboy.

After Conway took Miguel and Javier by the hand and walked off, Sara asked, "Are you two dating?"

"No, we're just friends."

Sara sighed dramatically. "Conway and I dated for a brief time."

"I know. You're Miss February." Isi enjoyed Sara's startled expression. If she recalled correctly, Miss February had a killer body but was also spoiled and demanding. "Conway and I talk a lot."

"He said he didn't want kids. That's why we broke up."

Isi had advised Conway to be up front about his feelings toward children before he got serious with any woman.

"I don't understand why he has such an aversion to kids. He seems comfortable with your boys," Sara said.

"That's because he's not responsible for them."

"Too bad. He'd make a great father."

Isi agreed. She thought back to all their talks but couldn't recall Conway ever revealing the reason behind his objection to fatherhood.

Sara dragged her gaze from Conway's retreating figure. "He's such a hottie."

That was Conway—making women's hearts throb all over southern Arizona. "I better go," Isi said. "Nice meeting you, Sara."

"You, too."

As Isi hurried to catch up with Conway and the boys, she wondered if spending time with the twins would show him that having children could actually strengthen a couple's relationship.

How would you know?

Fine. She didn't know if her theory was right or wrong, but couldn't a girl dream of finding a man who'd love her and be a loving father to her sons? The twins were Isi's whole world and she'd never take a chance on a man who didn't treat her sons as if they were his own.

Conway would never be that man, but it didn't hurt to pretend they were a family—for today anyway.

"YOU THINK THEY'LL sleep through the night?" Conway asked when Isi tiptoed from the boys' bedroom Saturday night.

"I hope so," she said. "Are you in a hurry, or do you have time to sit outside and drink a glass of lemonade?"

"I'm not in a rush to leave." Heck, his plans for the day had been shot a long time ago. He'd woken this morning, intending to take Isi and the boys to the carnival for a couple of hours, then head back to the farm to work. Instead, he'd spent the whole day with the little family. And he didn't understand why that didn't bother him more.

"Here you go." She handed him a plastic cup filled with pink lemonade and they went outside on the porch. They sat in silence, listening to crickets chirp. A breeze blew the faint scent of Isi's perfume past his nose, reminding him that he found her attractive, and nice and smart. And it depressed him. Why did all the perfect women either have kids or want them?

"Thank you for being kind to Miguel and Javier, Conway."

"They're good boys. You've done a great job raising them." He tapped his cup against hers. "To superhero moms."

"I was terrified when I brought the boys home from the hospital."

Conway gaped at Isi.

"What's the matter?" she asked.

"I just realized…"

"What?"

"I don't know much about you and your family."

"I didn't know you were interested in pecan farming. That took me by surprise." She winked and Conway felt an electric zap in his chest.

He cleared his throat. "I've always possessed a connection to the land but then I grew up and—" he flashed a grin "—became popular with the ladies and forgot all about pecans."

"What changed your mind about becoming more involved with the farm?"

"Johnny wasn't able to find an agricultural company to lease the orchards, so I stepped up and said I'd bring in this year's crop." He chugged the lemonade. "Time will tell if I'm able to turn a profit."

"Do you still plan to lease the groves?"

"Depends on how things go with the harvest." If the nuts brought in enough money to cover expenses, he was certain his siblings would approve of him taking over the farm on a permanent basis.

"Are your brothers helping you?"

"Nope. It's all on my shoulders."

"Isn't that going to cut into your rodeo schedule?" she asked.

Heck, it wasn't the orchards that interfered with rodeo—it was Isi and her sons. "I'll catch a rodeo here or there."

"Oh, dear." Her brow scrunched.

"What?"

"Missing all those rodeos is going to decrease your chances of finding *the one*."

"I suppose I'll have to hunt for my true love at farm auctions." He sobered. "You did it again."

"Did what?"

"Steered the subject back to me." He set his empty glass aside. "Tell me about your family."

"I don't like to talk about them."

"Why not?"

"Because when I block out the past, I'm less frightened of the future."

Her honesty caught Conway by surprise. He'd never pictured Isi as a woman intimidated by anything. "Tell me. Please."

After a long exhale, she said, "I was born in La Boca, a poor neighborhood in Buenos Aires, Argentina."

"Argentina? I assumed you were from Mexico."

She rolled her eyes. "One of the first things I learned coming to the Unites States was that most people assume anyone who speaks Spanish is from Mexico."

"Do you miss Argentina?" he asked.

"Yes, but I'd never go back."

"What happened to your family?"

"One morning my father went to work at the factory and he never came home. I was five years old. My twin brothers were eleven. My mother waited an entire week and when my father still hadn't returned, she took me with her to the police station to report him missing."

When Isi went silent, he asked, "Did they find your father?"

"No. It was as if he'd vanished into thin air. My mother was a housemaid for a well-to-do family but in order to cover our rent, she had to pick up a second job cleaning business offices at night. My brothers and I were left on our own."

"But you were only a year older than Miguel and Javier." Conway couldn't imagine leaving a young child home alone all day and night.

"Three or four months after my father disappeared, my mother received an eviction notice because she'd fallen behind on the rent. My brothers dropped out of school, joined a gang and sold drugs to help keep a roof over our heads."

"Your mother allowed your brothers to do that?"

"She wasn't the same after my father disappeared. She went through the motions for us kids but a part of her died when she lost my dad."

"How long were your brothers in the gang?"

"Almost four years. They'd bring me supper in the evenings and ask about my school day then take off again and spend the rest of the night on the streets."

"What happened to them?"

"I was nine when they didn't show up at the apartment with my supper. The next morning the police knocked on our door and told my mother that her sons had been gunned down in a drug raid."

Conway squeezed Isi's hand. "I'm sorry." Sorry didn't convey the hurt he felt for her.

"My mother cried for days, missing work at both her jobs. Then one morning she said, 'Isadora, you will stay in school and graduate.' Then we moved out of the apartment and rented a room in a boarding house, where I helped with chores in exchange for my meals."

"And you stayed in school?"

"I went to class every day and studied hard. I learned English and promised my mother that one day we would move to the U.S. and make a better life for ourselves. After I completed my education, I got a job tutoring students in English and I began saving money. Then my mother was hit by a bus on her way to work."

Conway couldn't find his voice to express his sympathy.

"There were a lot of pedestrian accidents in the city and my mother wasn't paying attention when she crossed against the light."

At eighteen Isi had been the only surviving member of her family. His chest physically ached as he envisioned her burying her mother next to her brothers and an empty grave for her father.

"I had an aunt and uncle who lived in Buenos Aires, but they didn't offer to take me in, so I packed my bags and came to the U.S. by myself."

"Your mother would be proud of you."

"I hope so."

"Are the twins named after their uncles?"

"Yes."

"The boys are lucky to have you for a mother. They're going to grow up to be fine men."

"I want them to have a good life and be happy."

"Mind if I ask who Miguel and Javier's father is?"

"Tyler Smith," she said.

"The bull rider?"

"That's him."

Smith was in his early thirties and was the construction foreman for Desert Builders—a company that competed against Will's boss for projects in the Yuma area.

"I'd gotten a work permit in the U.S. and began waitressing at the pancake house on Main Street when Tyler walked in after a rodeo and asked me out on a date." She sighed. "I knew he was trouble, but he was handsome and I was lonely."

Conway clenched his jaw, refusing to picture Isi with Tyler. "What did he say when you told him you were pregnant?"

"He insisted the baby wasn't his." Isi's soft brown eyes implored Conway to believe her. "I didn't cheat on Tyler."

"He's an ass." A surge of protectiveness filled Conway. Isi had no one to defend her and a part of him wanted to confront Smith and demand he do right by his sons.

"You know what?" she said. "All the times you've talked about your family, you've never mentioned your father."

"I told you that my brothers—"

"I know you were all fathered by different men, but how did growing up without a father affect you?"

"I never really gave it much thought." He hoped Isi wouldn't read the truth in his eyes. When he'd been a kid, Conway had thought about his father a lot. It wasn't until after he met the man that he quit thinking about him.

"Does it bother you that he wasn't involved in your life?" Isi asked.

"Not really." His standard response—the one he gave to avoid telling the truth.

"Right now the boys are young and they don't know any different because Tyler hasn't been involved in their life, but I worry that down the road they'll ask why he never visits."

The twins would ask. And when Isi's explanation wasn't good enough, her sons would go to bed at night feeling sick to their stomachs like Conway had.

"Javier is more sensitive than Miguel. I worry he'll believe there's something wrong with him and that's the reason Tyler doesn't visit." She nudged Conway's side. "Is that how you felt when your father stayed away?"

Conway didn't know how to address Isi's concern

without making her more anxious. It had bothered the hell out of Conway that his father hadn't wanted a relationship with him, but after meeting the man, he didn't see any point in getting to know him better. "I had my brothers and grandfather to make up for an absentee father."

"It's amazing the changes I've seen in the boys since you began watching them. Javier isn't as shy and Miguel is more cooperative." She finished her drink and set the cup aside. "Once I graduate and find a full-time professional job, I'll get back into dating. You've proven to me that the boys need a male in their lives."

"Don't rush into anything. It'd be worse for Javi and Mig if you date a guy and break up with him soon after."

"True, but there will come a time when I'm going to have to take a leap of faith."

Conway stood. He didn't care to discuss Isi's plans for her love life. "I better head to the farm."

She followed him to his truck. "Thanks for spending the day with us. I enjoyed the carnival as much as the boys did."

"See you on Monday." He offered a quick wave then drove off. The trip to the farm lasted forever as Isi's words rang through his head....

I'm going to have to take a leap of faith.

With his paternal family history a leap of faith was the worst thing Conway could take. After spending a week with Javier and Miguel he admitted that he enjoyed being with the twins, but he wasn't so naive as to assume the fun and newness wouldn't eventually wear off and be replaced by the heavier burden of responsibility. And then what? Would the itch to move on hit him?

As much as he might be tempted to open himself up to dating single mothers or women who wanted children, the risks were too great.

Chapter Six

Thursday night Isi marked off the last day in October on the calendar. November sure had taken its sweet time arriving. She'd been buried under midterm exams on top of waitressing at the bar, but it was more than school and work that had caused the days to crawl by—she and Conway hadn't spent much time together.

And she hadn't expected to miss him.

After Erica had left for California, Conway had been the only person she'd had regular contact with outside school and her job. Listening to Conway's girl troubles had made her feel connected to the real world. The two weeks that had passed since the carnival made her admit how alone she and the boys really were. She wished she could go back to the days when Conway swaggered into the bar after a rodeo and flashed his sexy grin. Now, she woke each morning to the boys chattering about the fun they'd had the previous day with Conway.

You're jealous.

She was jealous of her sons and wished she could switch places with them. She wanted to ride the tractor with Conway and learn how to shell pecans. She wanted to watch TV in the bunkhouse where Conway and his brothers slept. And she wanted to see Conway hold Dixie's son, Nathan, and stop him from crying.

Blast it, she wanted to see and experience all the things her sons had with Conway, but not once had he asked her to visit the farm. She didn't understand why he was pulling away from her, especially after the day they'd spent at the carnival. The heated looks they'd exchanged and Conway's accidental touches proved their attraction to one another was as strong and hot as it had been two years ago when they'd first met.

She wasn't foolish enough to believe she might be Conway's *the one,* but at the pace he was going, he might not find that woman for years. In the meantime, why couldn't they flirt? And if flirting led to sex…was that so terrible? She was a grown woman—a mother of four-year-old twins, whose sex life was as dry as the desert landscape outside the trailer. Didn't she deserve a night of steamy sex once in a blue moon? She'd never been promiscuous. The boy's father had only been the second man she'd slept with—the first had been her high school crush, but they'd been forced to break up when his parents discovered she lived in La Boca.

The twins were getting the best of Conway—why couldn't she have the best of him, too, for a short while?

"When's Conway gonna get here?" Miguel stood by the window.

"Soon," Isi said. Conway had offered to take Miguel and Javier trick-or-treating because Red had scheduled her to work at the bar tonight. When Sasha learned that Isi wouldn't be able to go trick-or-treating with the boys, she'd insisted on covering Isi's shift. Isi had texted Conway that he was off the hook, but he still wanted to go out with them.

She studied her son's costumes. The superpower duo had been decided upon months ago, making it easy for Isi to save the money and buy them before the stores sold out. Miguel was Captain America and Javier was the Green Lantern. "Let me take your picture." She grabbed the disposable camera and moved closer. "Smile." One day when she had the money, she intended to make a scrapbook using the photos she'd taken through the years and then add the few pictures she had of her brothers, mother and father, so the twins wouldn't forget their family.

"What are you, Mom?" Javier asked.

"I'm a sheriff, silly." She'd worn tight-fitting jeans and strapped the boys play pistol belt around her hips then pinned a sheriff's star to her long-sleeved Western shirt. Her straw cowboy hat and leather cowboy boots completed the outfit.

A knock on the trailer door sent the boys running across the room.

"Is that you, Conway?" Miguel shouted, his hand on the knob.

"It's me."

Miguel opened the door and Javier's face lit up with excitement. "What superhero are you, Conway?"

"I'm not a superhero, Javi. I'm a caveman."

Isi nearly swallowed her tongue when Conway stepped into the trailer wearing a fur cape. Her gaze traveled over his muscular bare chest, across his leatherlike kilt and down his naked legs—which she'd never seen before now—to the flip-flops on his feet.

"What's a caveman?" Miguel asked.

"A man who lives in a cave." Conway smiled.

Isi couldn't take her eyes off him. He'd thought of all the details—a battery-operated torch and armbands that showed off his biceps muscles. He'd spiked his sandy hair with gel, leaving the ends sticking up in all directions. He was the sexiest caveman she'd ever seen.

Fighting a smile she said, "For a cowboy you sure have tan legs."

"There's a swimming hole at the farm," he said.

"How come we don't get to go swimming?" Miguel asked.

"Because I don't know if you guys can swim."

"They've never had lessons," Isi said.

"Maybe next spring when the water warms up, I'll teach you two how to swim."

Isi winced at Conway's promise. Spring was a long way off and what if he found *the one* before the pond warmed up?

"Mom's a sheriff," Javier said.

Conway studied her outfit then he flashed a sexy grin and raised his hands in the air. "I surrender."

The boys giggled, but Isi wasn't laughing at the heat in Conway's eyes. She swallowed hard when she imagined his strong, naked legs entwined with hers on the bed in the room at the back of the trailer.

"Conway switched his attention to the boys. "What superheroes are you guys?"

"I'm Captain America," Miguel said, then motioned to his brother. "Javi's the Green Lantern."

"See?" Javier held out his hand.

Conway examined the plastic ring on Javi's finger. "What does it do?"

Miguel answered for his brother. "Javi has to think real hard and then he can make stuff happen."

"And Captain America can throw his shield and it'll come back to him," Javi said.

"You guys will give Superman a run for his money." Conway turned to Isi. "Ready to leave?"

"Let me take a picture." She'd buy double prints of the photo—one for the scrapbook and one for her nightstand drawer. "Move next to Conway." Isi snapped the photo. "Go fetch your candy bags." The boys raced to their room.

"Where do you usually trick-or-treat?" Conway asked. "In the trailer park?"

"Not many of the neighbors hand out candy, so I take the boys to the mall. Most of the merchants give out treats."

"I have a better idea. One of Dixie's friends lives a few miles away in a subdivision. We'll go there."

"Are you sure we're allowed to do that?"

"Dixie used to trick-or-treat there when she was younger."

"The boys would love to walk from house to house with other kids," she said. Once the twins returned with their bags, they piled into Conway's truck.

As they drove through town, Isi couldn't stop herself from admiring Conway's naked thighs and the way the muscles bunched when he pressed the brake or accelerator. She recalled the first time he walked into the bar and turned his smile on her—she'd almost fainted. And for a short while she'd lived in a fantasy world, believing Conway might be her "the one." Once she understood how strongly he opposed becoming a father, she'd accepted that they'd only ever be friends. Would he rethink his stance on fatherhood after helping her with the boys, or was she reading too much into the time he spent with them?

"Hey, Conway," Javier said.

"What?"

"When I grow up I'm gonna be a farmer like you."

Isi smiled.

"I'm gonna ride broncs like you," Miguel chimed in.

"When I grow up," Conway said. "I want to go to Tiny Tot Learn and Play like you guys."

The boys erupted in laughter, but Isi wasn't smiling. She stared out the window at the passing cars and second-guessed her decision to allow Conway to take care of her sons. She'd believed the boys would benefit from having a man in their lives, but she hadn't considered how the twins would react when Conway stopped coming by.

You'll have to find a man to replace him.

No one could replace Conway, but the idea had merit. If she had a boyfriend by the time she graduated, then when Conway quit babysitting, the twins wouldn't feel his loss as deeply.

Conway turned into a neighborhood and parked at the end of a block. "This is a good place to start." After they got out of the truck, he said, "You guys stick together. Don't walk off by yourself."

As they followed the boys, Isi whispered, "You'd better be careful, you're sounding like a father."

"Sorry, that slipped out."

"No need to apologize. You've been watching the boys almost a month. It's only natural for you to take charge." And surprisingly it didn't bother Isi that he took the lead with her sons. After four years of having sole responsibility for the twins, she enjoyed the brief respite.

Isi and Conway waited on the sidewalk as Miguel and Javier walked up to the first door. "Don't forget to say thank you," she called after them.

Miguel rang the bell and they hollered, "Trick-or-treat!" After receiving their candy they shouted a thank-you then cut across the lawn to the next house.

"The weather's beautiful tonight," she said, feeling nervous as she walked beside Conway.

"You can't beat southern Arizona in the fall." Conway set his hand against her lower back and guided her through a crowd of kids. They continued walking, but he didn't remove his hand, and Isi's pulsed raced as the skin beneath his touch warmed.

"You look hot in your sheriff's getup," he whispered in her ear.

"I bet you say that to all the ladies." She forced a smile. "Speaking of ladies…we haven't talked about your latest 'the one.'"

"Who's that?"

She shrugged. "I assumed you'd found a new woman."

"Between watching the boys and working on the farm I haven't had time to date."

They strolled to the next house in silence, Isi lost in thought. She'd been so relieved when Conway had volunteered to take care of the boys while she finished out the semester that she hadn't given a thought to how it would affect his personal life. "I'll keep searching for a permanent sitter."

"Why?"

"Because you said you don't have any time to yourself."

"Neither do you."

"I'm not supposed to. I'm a single mother."

"Mom!" Javier raced toward her, holding out his bag. "The lady gave us a giant candy bar."

"She sure did." Isi waved at the woman. "Did you thank her?"

"Yep." Miguel pointed to the house at the end of street where a large crowd of kids gathered. "She said that man gives out lot of treats to kids who don't get scared and run away."

"It's a haunted house," Isi said.

Miguel tugged his brother's arm. "C'mon, Javi."

The boys ran off and Isi and Conway both called, "Stay together!"

"We'd better catch up." Conway took Isi's hand and they walked fast, keeping the boys in sight.

"This guy went all out," Conway said.

Ghosts hung from tree branches. Skulls and skeletal hands stuck out of the ground next to tombstones. The dark porch was filled with cobwebs and scary music blasted from an open window. The front door had been covered in white butcher paper with the words *Keep Out* painted in red.

The boys were at the back of the line, so Isi settled in for a long wait. "You've more than made up for Bridget punching me in the nose, Conway. There's no reason your love life should suffer any longer."

The heat in his eyes burned the side of her neck. "Is that all you think I care about—having sex?"

The group of women standing nearby stopped talking. Isi lowered her voice. "C'mon, Conway. It's me, Isi, you're talking to. Finding 'the one' has been your main preoccupation since we met two years ago."

"Hey, a guy's entitled to take a break from romance every now and then."

She snorted.

"I'm not a stud machine who can switch on and off, you know."

"I'm still going to try to find a sitter."

They stood for a few more minutes, watching the fray of kids then Conway stiffened next to her. "I see Miguel, but where's Javier?" He didn't wait for Isi to respond before charging up the sidewalk. "Javi?" he shouted.

Miguel raced toward Conway.

"Where's Javi, Mig?" Isi asked when she caught up.

"He was next to me when the man gave us candy."

"Did he go inside the house, Miguel?" Conway asked.

"No, the man didn't open the door."

Conway noticed a hand poked through the hole in the paper that covered the door and dropped candy into the waiting bags." He glanced down the block. "I'll follow that group. You two stay here in case Javier comes back."

Heart racing, Conway caught up to the mass of goblins and fairies. One by one he surveyed the kids' costumes but didn't see a Green Lantern in the group. Panic squeezed his gut. Javier had most likely gotten swallowed up by a wave of kids as they passed by him.

Where are you, Javi?

If Conway hadn't suggested trick-or-treating in a larger neighborhood, the boy wouldn't have gotten lost. He reached the end of the block then called Javier's name.

"Excuse me. Did you lose your child?" A woman pushing a stroller approached Conway.

"Yes, ma'am. He's wearing a green superhero costume. Have you seen him?"

"I'm sorry, I haven't." She motioned to a crowd up the block. "That's our church group. We'll keep an eye out for him."

"Thanks. His name's Javier." Conway jogged ahead of the group and caught the next crowd. "Has anyone seen a kid wearing a Green Lantern costume?"

The children shook their heads and Conway's chest felt as though it would explode from fear. There was no way Javier could have walked much farther. When he turned the next corner, he spotted a woman standing on a front lawn, holding Javier's hand.

Thank God. He hurried toward them. When Javier noticed him, he raced to Conway.

Weak with relief Conway dropped to one knee on the sidewalk and hugged the boy. "I'm glad you're okay, buddy."

"I told him that his mother or father would find him." The lady held the hand of a ballerina in a pink tutu.

"Thank you for watching out for him," Conway said.

"Stay by your father now." The lady smiled then walked off with her daughter.

Conway was so relieved he'd found Javier unharmed that he didn't care if the woman thought they were father and son. "Why did you leave your brother?"

Javier squeezed Conway's neck and sobbed.

"Whoa, buddy. You're safe now."

"I didn't run off." Javier's chest shuddered when he took a deep breath. "Mig left me."

"Mig didn't leave you, Javi. He's still back at the haunted house."

"I couldn't see him."

"It's all right. All that matters is you're safe. Let's find your mom." Instead of holding Javier's hand, Conway scooped him off the ground and carried him. As his heart rate slowed, his thoughts raced. The boy had been lucky tonight—he could have been abducted by a crazy pedophile. Losing track of Javier was more proof that Conway wasn't meant to be a father. He just couldn't handle the responsibility or worry that came with keeping kids safe.

As he drew closer to the haunted house, Isi hurried toward them. "Javi, where were you?"

Conway set the boy on the ground and Javi shoved Miguel. "You left me!"

"No, I didn't!" Miguel pushed Javier back and the boys tumbled to the ground.

Conway snagged the backs of their costumes, holding them apart while their tiny fists pummeled the air.

"Stop right now or we go home," Isi said.

"You left me," Miguel said.

"Did not!"

"Did, too!"

"We're done for the night." Isi took Javier's hand and motioned for Conway to hold Miguel's, but the kid crossed his arms over his chest and marched off behind his mother and brother.

Conway followed. After a block Miguel whispered, "I didn't leave, Javi."

"It's easy to lose track of each other in a crowd," Conway said.

"It's not fair."

"What's not fair?" Conway slowed his steps so their conversation wouldn't be overheard by Isi and Javier.

"Mom always makes me take care of Javi."

Conway felt bad for Miguel. He had to find a way to salvage the night. Halloween came once a year and he hated for the boys to go home mad at each other with only a handful of candy in their bags.

When they reached the truck, the twins hopped in back, refusing to speak to each other. Conway pulled away from the curb and said, "I've got an idea."

"What's that?" Isi asked.

"Have the boys ever been to a drive-in theater?"

"What's a drive-in theater?" Miguel asked.

"A place you can watch movies in your car." Conway shrugged. "We could see what's playing?"

"But a movie rewards them for being naughty," Isi said.

"Maybe you could put off their punishment until to-morrow?" Conway pointed to the boys. "They look so sad."

Isi almost laughed when her sons' mouths pouted and they batted their eyelashes at her. "If we go to the movie that means no TV tomorrow. Understood?"

The twins nodded.

By the time Conway backed into a parking spot at the rear of the drive-in the second movie was beginning—*Invasion of the Spiders*. He helped the boys out of their booster seats then lifted them into the truck bed.

"I can't hear anything," Miguel complained.

Conway turned on the outdoor speakers.

"Cool," Miguel said.

"Yeah, cool." Javier smiled at his brother and the boys were back to being best friends.

"Who wants popcorn?" Conway asked.

The twins raised their hands.

"What kind of sodas?" Conway asked Isi.

"No soda. They can share a bottle of water."

Conway left to buy the snacks, and when he returned the twins were lying down and Isi leaned against the cab at the back of the truck bed. He crawled over the boys and joined Isi. They shared a bag of popcorn in silence. It wasn't long before her sons dozed off, and Conway watched Isi instead of the movie. Without thinking, he tucked a strand of hair behind her ear.

"I've never been to a drive-in," she said.

"Really?"

"I'm guessing you've broken your fair share of hearts in the back row."

"You'd guess wrong. You're the first woman I've been with at a drive-in."

"No way."

"Yes way. I've been here twice with my brothers when we were younger and once with Dixie after she coerced me into taking her and a group of her junior high friends."

"I'm your first official drive-in date?" she asked.

"Yes, ma'am."

"You were always the one who did most of the talking in our relationship," Isi said. "Now I need your advice."

"Sure."

"After my experience with Tyler, I've avoided dating, believing I was better off raising the boys on my own."

"I sense a *but* coming," he said.

"But seeing how happy Javi and Mig are after they spend time with you…" She took a deep breath. "Do I need to get out there and start dating again?"

Conway felt a stitch in his side and winced. "It doesn't matter what I think. You have to do what's best for you and the boys."

"What if I date a guy I like, but the boys don't like him? That could be a disaster. Maybe I should focus on finding a man who wants to be friends but enjoys being with the boys."

"You know what?" Conway said. "You're nothing like the women I date."

She laughed. "You just figured that out?"

"Seriously. The women I end up with only think about themselves. You think about the boys."

"I'm their mother, Conway. The boys will always come first."

"I understand you wanting the best for Mig and Javi, but what if after a while the guy wants more than friendship from you?"

"That would be great," she said, surprising Conway.

"I'm only telling you this because we're friends and you won't blab to anyone." She leaned closer. "I haven't had sex since I got pregnant with the boys."

Wow.

"I'm in a four-year drought and right now sex with a guy friend seems mighty appealing."

Conway couldn't shake the image of a faceless man stripping Isi of her clothes.

"It's time I find a man who'll be good for the boys and for me."

Conway didn't think that was a smart idea at all. "You're the boss," he said, reluctantly.

"What do you mean?"

He tapped the plastic star on her shirt. "You're in charge."

"You're right. A sheriff calls the shots." She smiled. "It's not like I haven't had offers." She'd been hit on at the bar a number of times. The heat radiating off Conway's body interfered with her concentration. She scooted over until his bare thigh no longer brushed against her leg.

"Aren't you concerned about how the twins will react if you bring home a boyfriend?" Conway asked.

"Not anymore."

"What changed your mind?"

"You."

"Me? What did I do?"

"The boys love being with you. It's obvious they're starved for male attention."

"Whatever guy you date isn't going to be me."

She punched him playfully in the arm. "You're full of yourself."

"Hey, I'm being honest."

"I'm guessing the boys will measure any man I date

against you and find him lacking, but you're not going to be here forever." She snapped her fingers. "Maybe I should date behind the boys' backs until I find the right man to introduce to them to."

"That's a good idea." Conway grinned despite his reservations. "I wouldn't want your new man to jeopardize my rock-star status with Javi and Mig."

Chapter Seven

The first week of November was drawing to a close. Conway stood in the pecan orchard and peered into the canopy of a tree.

"What are we looking for?" Javier asked.

"I'm not sure." Conway had followed his grandfather through the groves many times and every few trees he'd stop and study the leafy branches—as if he sensed which ones would yield the most nuts. Conway checked over his shoulder, making sure Miguel remained in sight. That kid was definitely not a farmer. He couldn't stand or sit still for more than a few minutes, unlike Javier who had the patience of Job and did whatever Conway asked of him.

"What do you think, Javi? Is this tree going to drop a lot of nuts when I bring the shaker machine through?"

"I don't see any nuts."

Conway lifted the boy above his head. "Grab hold of that branch and climb up."

"Me, too!" Miguel raced toward Conway.

Once Javier had settled on a limb, Conway said "Don't fall." The last thing he wanted to do was call Isi and tell her that one of the boys had broken an arm or leg.

Miguel impatiently hopped up and down, waiting hi

turn. Conway hoisted him into the tree. "Pick a branch and count the nuts on it."

The boys called out different numbers. After a few seconds, they counted in unison. Javier stumbled at fifty, but Miguel corrected him and they continued until they reached a hundred.

"There's got to be more than a hundred nuts on that branch," Conway said. The boys ignored him and started a pecan war.

"Hey!" Conway said when he felt a nut ping his head.

The boys giggled as they bombarded each other. Conway scooped a fistful of nuts off the ground and joined the battle. The twins combined forces against Conway and he shouted, "No throwing at the face!" As soon as he turned his back to gather more ammunition, the boys pelted his butt with nuts. "You'll pay for that."

"Who are you talking to?" Isi walked toward Conway, her gaze scanning the trees.

"Where'd you come from?" Conway couldn't stop staring at her tight-fitting jeans—the ones that hugged her fanny to perfection and sported tiny tears in the thighs.

"My class was canceled." She shrugged. "So I drove out here to see my favorite guys before I go to work." The warmth in her brown eyes convinced Conway that he was included in Isi's group of favorite guys.

"Where are the boys?" She stopped next to him.

"Up here." Miguel poked his head through the branches.

Isi moved closer but froze when a pecan flew past her face. "Miguel! You better not throw any nuts at me, young man."

The boys scrambled to a lower branch and Conway lifted them out of the tree and set them on the ground.

Isi threw a pecan at Miguel, hitting him in the chest then she tossed a nut at Javier. "Got you both."

Miguel collected ammunition from the ground and Conway handed the nuts he'd collected to Javier.

"No fair." Isi ran off, dodging pecans as the boys chased her through the trees.

"Don't let her get away!" Conway jogged after the group.

The boys' laughter and Isi's squeals filled the groves, reminding Conway of days gone by when he and his siblings had played tag in the orchard. It wasn't long before the twins ran out of gas and stopped, their chests heaving as they sucked in air. Isi bent at the waist, gasping for breath.

"I'm out of shape." She laughed.

"We helped Conway count pecans," Javier said.

"And I helped rake the branches." Miguel neglected to tell his mother that he'd raked for two minutes before handing the chore over to his brother.

"You guys go ask Porter for a drink of water," Conway said.

"C'mon, Javi, maybe we can share Porter's Skittles." The boys raced to the bunkhouse.

Isi watched her sons run off. "I thought bunkhouses were like big log cabins not giant metal sheds."

"The Cash brothers aren't your traditional cowboys." He grinned.

She scuffed the toe of her shoe in the dirt and he had a hunch she hadn't dropped by the farm for a visit.

"What's on your mind?" he asked.

"I need a favor."

"What kind of favor?"

"Would you be willing to stay later than usual tonight to watch the boys?"

"Got a hot date?"

"As a matter of fact, I do."

A sudden coldness gripped his chest. "Really?"

"Yes, really." Frowning, she said, "I told you I wanted to start dating again."

He thought she'd been venting in the back of his pickup Halloween night. "Who are you going out with?"

"Sean Mason."

"The name doesn't sound familiar. Does he rodeo?"

"I'm not sure. Sasha set me up with him. He's been to the bar a few times."

"What else do you know about this guy? You can't be too careful these days," he said.

"Thank you for being concerned, but I can handle myself."

"Sure, I'll watch the boys." He planned to grill *Sean* after he dropped Isi off.

"Thanks."

The bunkhouse door opened and Javier and Miguel stepped outside, their pockets bulging with candy. "You two be good for Conway." Isi kissed their cheeks. "And don't forget to brush your teeth tonight."

"They'll brush twice." Conway laughed when the twins groaned.

After Isi drove away, he got the weirdest feeling in his gut. He didn't like the idea of her dating a guy she barely knew.

Or maybe he didn't like the idea of Isi dating—period.

THIS DATE WAS a bust.

"You wanna dance?" Sean Mason asked.

I'd rather call it a night. Conway would have pulled

out the chair for her, but Sean walked off, expecting her to follow him to the dance floor.

The Desert Lounge in Yuma was a popular dance club where local bands performed for free. The Rattlers provided tonight's entertainment and the middle-aged trio—two guitar players and a drummer—sang country music from days gone by. Sean stopped in the middle of the floor and pulled Isi into his arms, then twirled her in circles. *Show off.*

Once her head stopped spinning, she struggled not to squirm. Nothing felt right about Sean. He was too short. She didn't like the spicy scent of his cologne. His hands were soft. And he rarely smiled.

He's not Conway.

The song ended and the lead singer cleared his throat, the gravelly sound rumbling through the speakers on the stage. "We got any Conway Twitty fans out there tonight?"

Isi's gaze flew to the exit, hoping for the impossible—Conway waltzing through the door.

"Hold your ladies close, cowboys—" the musician grinned "—because…'It's Only Make Believe.'"

When Sean pulled Isi closer, she braced her palm against his shoulder and locked her elbow to keep their bodies from rubbing against each other. What had possessed her to let Sasha set her up on a date?

Conway.

She'd wanted to prove her feelings for Conway were those of a girl with a teenage crush and nothing more. The only thing tonight had established was that she'd rather be with Conway.

A couple bumped into Sean's back and Isi cringed when their lower bodies came in contact and she felt the bulge in his jeans. If the cowboy expected her to invite him into her bed, he was in for a big surprise.

After the song ended, the band took a break, but Sean made no move to leave the dance floor. A quarter found its way into the jukebox and they continued dancing. Isi made a second attempt at conversation. "Sasha said you're a wrangler at a local ranch.

"The Flying S." He didn't elaborate.

Sean hadn't strung more than two sentences together the entire night. Each time she asked him a personal question, he changed the subject. When she attempted to talk about her classes at school, he cut her off and argued that too much education made a person uppity. Who used the word *uppity* anymore? "Any vacation plans for Christmas?"

He shook his head.

She gave up trying to salvage the date. When the song ended, Sean headed back to their table. She'd finished her beer an hour ago, but he hadn't offered to buy her a second. The time on her cell phone showed midnight.

"I better get home," she said. The boys would be up early in the morning.

Without a word, Sean led the way outside to the parking lot. He hopped into his truck—again not bothering to open the passenger side door for her.

No wonder women fawned all over Conway—he was a true gentleman and knew how to treat a lady.

Sean drove Isi to the Border Town Bar & Grill where she'd left her car. As soon as he shifted the truck into park, she opened her door and flashed a quick smile. No sense lying and telling him she'd enjoyed their date. "Night."

She caught a glimpse of his surprised face as she shut

the door. Too bad if he expected a good-night kiss—Conway was the only man she wanted to smooch with. She got into her car and the headlights from Sean's truck moved across her back window when he left the lot.

As Isi drove home, she decided that finding a nice guy to fill the void in her and the boys' lives was going to be more difficult than she thought.

CONWAY PEERED BETWEEN the blinds in the front window of Isi's trailer. He'd put the boys to bed five hours ago then watched a marathon of *Hawaii Five-0* shows on TV. If he heard "Book 'em, Danno" one more time, he'd throw his boot at the wall.

One in the morning. Pretty soon the bars would close down, then where would they go—back to Mason's apartment? Isi was a good mother. She worked hard at school and her job. She deserved to be happy, but not too happy—at least until the end of the semester when his nanny services would no longer be needed.

Isi sleeping with a man bothered him.

No. Yes. Conway's stomach growled. He went into the kitchen and surveyed the contents of the fridge. A few apples and oranges. A plastic container of leftovers. Two gallons of milk and a variety of condiments. The freezer contained a box of waffles, a bag of French fries and a tub of cheap ice cream.

He moved to the cupboards, finally settling on SpaghettiOs and eating them cold from the can. Finished with his snack he stepped outside and sat on the porch. He dug his cell phone from his pocket for the umpteenth time and checked for messages—none. He was positive that if Isi went to a motel with Mason, she'd let him know she wouldn't be home until morning. Be sides, she wasn't the kind of woman to sleep with a guy on the first date.

How do you know? She hasn't had sex in four years.

A pair of headlights turned into the mobile-home park. Conway bolted back inside and switched the TV on so she wouldn't know he'd paced the floor waiting for her. He peeked out the window and watched her park beneath the carport. Why hadn't Mason followed her to make sure she'd gotten home safe?

The trailer door opened and Isi stepped inside.

Conway noticed her neat hair and clothes. Her lips weren't even swollen. He hadn't realized he'd been holding his breath until it whooshed from his body.

"What are you smiling at?" She set her purse on the table.

Unwilling to examine why her neat appearance made him happy, he rubbed a hand down his face, erasing his grin. "How was your date?"

Her eyes shimmered with tears.

Uh-oh. "I take it the evening didn't go well."

"Hardly." She made a move to pass by him, but he snagged her arm.

She looked so dejected he couldn't help himself— he hugged her. "I'm sorry, Isi." He wasn't really. "What happened?"

"Sean was a jerk."

"You want me to beat him up for you?" he said, hoping to coax a smile out of her.

"No." She wrapped her arms around his waist and snuggled closer. "I never got my good-night kiss."

Don't even think about it. But that's all he'd done tonight—imagined Isi kissing her date. Ignoring the voice in his head warning him not to overstep his bounds, Conway tilted her chin until she made eye contact with him.

"What are you doing?" she whispered.

"Giving you a good-night kiss." The scent of faded perfume and warm woman surrounded him, drawing his mouth closer to hers. He hesitated, waiting to see if she'd pull away. She didn't.

He held himself back, keeping the first press of his mouth against her lips light and gentle, reacquainting himself with their flavor. Their softness. When her mouth relaxed beneath his, he eased his tongue inside and tasted her.

She swayed closer, her fingers fluttered over his ribs. A groan rumbled through his chest when her small breasts flattened against him. Could she feel his heart pound?

He was playing with fire, but he relished the burn and deepened the kiss. She didn't shy away. Instead, she grew bolder, engaging in a game of dueling tongues that robbed him of oxygen. He had to end this insanity before he lifted her into his arms and carried her into the bedroom.

He broke off the kiss and stepped back. She stared wide-eyed, pressing her fingers against her moist lips. Neither said a word for the longest time, then she asked, "Do you kiss all your first dates like that?"

"Sorry, I got carried away." He sensed Isi would have allowed him get a lot carried away if he'd wanted to.

Needing a moment to gather her wits, Isi walked into the kitchen and got a drink of water. Good Lord, Conway's kiss had sucked all the oxygen out of her, leaving her light-headed. She set the empty cup in the sink and faced him. "I'm not giving up." There had to be a man whose kiss could rock her world the way Conway's had.

"Just because Sean turned out to be a dud doesn't mean the next guy will be one, too. I'll ask Sasha if she—"

"After tonight I wouldn't trust Sasha to find you a date," he said.

"I need a friend to set me up, because I'm not the kind of girl who asks guys out."

"I'll find you a date," Conway said.

"Seriously?"

He nodded.

"It would be nice to go on a date before Thanksgiving."

"Done."

She didn't know whether to be miffed or appreciative that Conway was eager to push her off on another guy. "No jerks."

"Don't worry. The man I find for you will be harmless."

HE WAS IN TROUBLE. *Big trouble.*

Conway sped down the highway toward Stagecoach, putting as many miles between him and the Desert Valley Mobile Home Park as fast as possible.

He'd been a fool to kiss Isi, but her sad eyes had begged him to erase the bad memory of her date with jerk Mason.

Don't blame Mason. You've been waiting for an excuse to kiss Isi for a long time.

He clenched the wheel tighter until his knuckles ached. He'd wanted to kiss Isi since he'd begun watching the twins. It wasn't a big deal. He'd kissed her before—

A long time ago.

Maybe, but he hadn't forgotten how great that kiss had been.

You got it out of your system, now forget it.

Easier said than done. Their kiss tonight had proven that the attraction he'd felt for Isi the first time he'd met her hadn't faded with time as he'd believed.

Why Isi? She'd be the perfect woman for him—if she didn't have the twins. He felt sorry for the boys growing up without a dad. Conway knew what it felt like and he wished differently for the boys. It was because he felt protective of Isi and her sons that he wanted to find her a decent man.

You mean possessive, not protective.

The damned voice in his head playing devil's advocate irritated the hell out of him.

Conway ran through a mental list of his rodeo buddies not sure who he could trust with Isi. They were good guys, but they were rodeo cowboys—anything could happen. There had to be a man who'd treat Isi like a lady and not push her into doing more than she was ready for.

Will.

Finally the voice in his head had said something worth listening to.

Why not his older brother? Will had quit chasing after buckle bunnies years ago. He was older than Isi, mature and harmless. He'd treat her right and show her a good time without coming on strong.

Problem solved. Now all he had to do was convince Will to go along with his plan.

SUNDAY MORNING CONWAY poked his head inside the bunkhouse door. Will sat at the table, leafing through the Home Depot ads while Buck and Porter played a game of chess. "Hey, Will, you got a second?"

"Sure." Will scooted his chair back then stepped outside. "What's up?"

"I have a favor to ask." Conway motioned for his brother to follow him to the barn where they could talk in private.

"Let me guess." Will chuckled. "You've got too many women chasing after you and you want me take one of them off your hands?"

Conway skidded to a stop. "How'd you know?"

Will sobered. "I was joking."

After they entered the barn, Conway took a seat at the workbench. "You're not dating anyone, are you?"

Will leaned against the tractor tire and crossed his arms over his chest. "No."

"I want you to take a friend of mine on a date."

"I'm almost thirty-four, Conway. I quit dating buckle bunnies a long time ago."

"That's why you're the perfect date for this woman."

Will narrowed his eyes. "What's wrong with her?"

"Nothing. She doesn't have time to meet guys, because she works, goes to school and she's a single—"

"Oh, no." Will shoved away from the tractor. "If you're referring to that gal from the Border Town Bar & Grill then—"

"Isi's a great catch." Conway stood and paced in front of his brother.

"If she's so perfect, you date her."

"I can't."

"Why not?"

Conway leveled a meaningful glare at his brother. His siblings knew how he felt about being a father.

"Oh, yeah. You won't date her because of the twins."

Bingo.

"How old is Isi?" Will asked.

"Twenty-four."

"She's way too young for me."

"Johnny married Shannon, and he's nine years her senior. Besides, Isi acts older than her age. She's responsible, independent and—"

"Forget it."

Conway went on as if Will hadn't spoken. "Isi had a date with a jerk the other night and now she's down in the dumps."

"Then you take her out and cheer her up," Will said. "You don't want kids but that doesn't mean you can't date a single mother."

His brother's suggestion made Conway squirm.

"You like her, don't you?" Will said.

"Of course I like her. She's a great person."

"But you're afraid to date her, because you might start liking her too much."

"Quit trying to psychoanalyze me. It's better for both Isi and me if we remain friends." Conway shoved his fingers through his hair. "I want you to make her feel special for one night."

Will quirked an eyebrow. "How special?"

"Not *that* special." Conway scowled. "C'mon, Will. You owe me."

"Owe you, how?"

"You never help on the farm, so you can pay me for all the work I—"

"Watch yourself, buddy." Will motioned to the bunkhouse visible through the open barn doors. "I built that without much help from you or Porter. I think we're even." Will walked away. "Ask Porter to take her out. He's easy-going and gets along with anyone."

Conway dogged his brother's heels. "Porter's too immature for Isi."

"When do you plan to harvest the pecans?"

"Around Thanksgiving. Quit changing the subject."

Conway tugged his brother's shirtsleeve. "You're the only one I trust to not take advantage of Isi."

"Fine." Will jerked his arm free. "I'll take her out next Friday."

"She doesn't get off work until midnight," Conway said.

Will's mouth dropped open.

"I know it's late, but can't you pick her up at the bar after her shift and go for a bite to eat?"

"Whatever. We'll figure it out. Give Isi my cell number in case she gets off earlier."

"Thanks, Will. I knew you'd come through for me."

As soon as his brother went inside the bunkhouse, Conway phoned Isi and left her a message. Now that he knew she'd be in good hands, he could relax and stop worrying.

Chapter Eight

"Hey, quiet down in there and go to sleep," Isi hollered from the kitchen Sunday night. She and the boys had spent most of the day outside, and she didn't understand how they weren't tired after all that fresh air.

She'd finished drying the last of the supper dishes when she heard a faint jingle. She cocked her head, trying to identify the noise. She'd heard the same muffled sound earlier in the day, but had been too busy chasing after the boys and doing chores to think much of it.

Cell phone.

Good grief, she'd left her cell in her backpack by the front door. She rummaged through the bag and discovered Conway had left her a voicemail message.

Her heart gave a little jolt. No matter how hard she'd tried to keep busy, she hadn't been able to forget the kiss she and Conway had shared last night. She dialed her inbox and listened to his deep voice.

"I've got a surprise for you," he said.

What kind of surprise?

"You're going on a date Friday night."

I am? She held her breath.

"I set you up with my brother, Will."

The excitement fizzled out of Isi. *Thanks, but I can find my own date.*

"Will's going to pick you up after your shift at work."

She had a whole week to think about dating Conway's brother. *Yee-haw.*

"Here's Will's cell number in case you get off early from work on Friday."

While Conway repeated the number, it occurred to Isi that he really didn't want to start anything between them. She'd been an idiot to hope that their kiss meant more to Conway than it did. It was probably best they stayed friends since she already knew how he felt about being a father.

"Will's a great guy, Isi. He'll enjoy hearing about the boys and the classes you're taking at the community college."

She racked her brain, trying to recall conversations she'd had with Conway about Will, but he'd talked mostly about Johnny—the eldest Cash brother who Conway idolized.

"Call me if you can't go out with Will Friday night. See you tomorrow."

End of messages.

Isi set the phone on the kitchen table. She'd go out with Will if only to stop Conway's meddling.

LATE FRIDAY NIGHT Isi sat in a booth across from Conway's brother at the All-American Diner in Yuma and ignored the butterflies fluttering in her stomach. She'd been a nervous wreck since Will had picked her up at the bar. And she had no one to blame but herself for her anxiety. Will was a polite, well-mannered, handsome man—exactly the kind of guy she wanted to date.

But he's not Conway.

"I hear my brother's a regular at the Border Town Bar & Grill," Will said.

"I've known Conway almost two years." She forced a smile, hoping Will would stop talking about his brother.

"I think we should get it out of the way," Will said.

"Get what out of the way?"

He leaned over the table, his mouth closing in on Isi's. Caught by surprise, she froze. A moment later, his lips pressed against hers. The kiss was warm and firm. Squeezing her eyes closed she analyzed the feel of Will's mouth against hers. There was no zing, zip or zap like she felt when Conway kissed her. The breath she'd been holding in her lungs escaped in a dramatic sigh and she opened her eyes to Will's devilish grin.

He cocked his head. "Nothing?"

Startled by his bluntness she answered honestly. "No."

"Didn't think so. My loss."

She laughed. "You're too much of a gentleman to admit that you didn't feel any sparks, either."

"Now that we got the kiss out of the way, we can relax and enjoy ourselves."

The queasiness Isi had felt since Will had picked her up at the bar magically disappeared. "I'm sorry you were coerced into taking me out tonight, but Conway's determined to find a man for me."

"Hmm."

"What?" She noticed a sparkle in his eye.

"I'm trying to figure out why Conway's so invested in your love life." Will frowned. "You're sure you two are only good friends?"

"Sure." She dropped her gaze.

"C'mon, Isi. Tell me the truth."

Face flushing, she said, "Conway and I hit it off when we first met, but—"

"Then he found out you had the twins."

"Yes."

"How well did you two hit it off?"

"Well enough." She resisted the urge to press her fingers against her burning cheeks.

"Did you kiss?"

"We shared a few kisses."

Will grinned.

"But nothing happened after that," she protested.

"Tell me if I've got this right," he said. "You two were attracted to each other. You kissed a few times, maybe several. And you were working your way toward the bedroom when he found out you were a single mother. Then he backed off and you settled for being friends."

"Wow. You're good."

"After all this time being friends, what rocked the status quo between you two?"

Will wasn't going to drop the subject, so Isi spilled the details of her date with Sean and how Conway had kissed her later that night, because he'd felt sorry for her.

"I think I know what's going on." Will's smile stretched into a full grin.

The waitress arrived with the food, halting their discussion. After she promised to return with drink refills, Will spoke. "Conway wants you for himself, but he's afraid things might get serious between the two of you and—"

"That wouldn't be good," she said. "Because Conway doesn't want to be a father."

"You nailed it."

"I like Conway a lot." Her feelings went deeper than "like" but she was afraid to voice them. "And I don't want to lose his friendship."

"Hate to break it to you—" Will shoveled a forkful of omelet into his mouth, chewed then swallowed. "As soon as Conway finds the perfect woman, she'll put a stop to his visits to the Border Town Bar & Grill when she finds out you're the reason he goes there."

Isi hadn't considered how Conway's "the one" might feel about her friendship with him. The thought of him not visiting her wherever she worked in the future depressed her. She changed the subject. "Conway said you're thirty-three."

"And still single."

"Confirmed bachelor or playing the field?" she asked.

"I don't play the field anymore, but I haven't found the right woman yet." He sipped his water. "I proposed to a woman a few years back but things didn't work out."

"Conway never mentioned anything about you or any of his brothers being engaged."

"My brothers didn't know about it," he said.

"What happened?"

"The night I'd proposed, I had a dream about a girl I'd gone on a date with my senior year in high school." He shook his head. "Craziest thing. After that dream I couldn't get her out of my head."

"Did you try to contact the girl?"

"No. We have nothing in common. The last I heard she was living in California."

"But the memory of this girl was enough to break things off with your fiancée?"

"I'm afraid so."

"I'm a believer in fate," Isi said. "Things happen for a reason."

"Maybe, but I also believe we control our own destinies," Will said. "I hear you've been working your way through college and you have a job. That's no easy feat with twins."

"I've had help along the way," she said. "My boss

has been great about adjusting my work schedule so I can take the classes I need to graduate. And when my babysitter moved out of town, Conway offered to watch the boys." She smiled. "They love being with him."

The diner waitress returned with their drinks then asked if they needed anything before she disappeared again.

"It's because of Conway that I decided I should start dating. The boys need a male role model in their lives."

"Speaking from experience, I'd wished my father would have wanted to be involved in my life."

"Conway spoke highly of your grandfather," she said.

"Grandpa Ely was a good man, but it was Johnny we all turned to as we grew older. He kept us in line and taught us how to defend ourselves against the bullies."

"I'm envious of you and your brothers," she said.

"Why's that? You always wanted to fight six siblings to use the bathroom?"

"I've dreamed of being part of a large family." She shrugged. "It's just me and my sons."

"You've got a lot going for you, Isi. You'll find a man who'll love your sons as much as you do."

They finished their meals in silence and Isi ordered coffee instead of dessert. "Conway mentioned you work in construction. Do you do any handyman work on the side?"

"Need a few repairs?"

"There are always things that need to be fixed in the trailer. My elderly landlord charges me next to nothing for rent, so I don't pester her about sticky windows and leaky faucets."

"I'll stop by your place next week," he said.

"That would be great." She smiled. "Thanks."

When they ran out of things to talk about, Isi pulled out her cell phone and said, "Oh, dear."

"What?"

"Conway sent a text message an hour ago, asking when we'd be back." She texted him saying they were on their way. Will drove her to the bar to pick up her car then followed her to her trailer.

When Will got out of his truck, she said, "You were a good sport tonight. I enjoyed getting to know you."

"Me, too, Isi. You're easy to talk to." He followed her up the porch steps.

When she walked into the trailer, Conway said, "'Bout time you got home."

Will ignored his brother's comment and spoke to Isi. "Dixie and Shannon are putting on a big spread for Thanksgiving. You and the boys should come out to the farm and spend the day with us."

"That's nice of you to offer, but we couldn't interfere in a family—"

"You won't be interfering," Will said. "Besides, it will give me a chance to get to know the twins better."

Conway's mouth sagged. Isi smothered a laugh behind a fake cough then said, "If you're sure, the boys and I would love to come."

"Great."

"Thanks again for the nice evening," Isi said.

"See you next week." Will closed the door behind him.

"What did he mean he'll see you next week?" Conway asked.

"Will offered to fix a few things around the trailer," she said.

"Why didn't you ask me for help?"

"I didn't think you did home repairs." The glower on his face worried her. "Did the boys misbehave tonight?"

"No, they were fine." Conway's gaze zeroed in on her mouth.

Was he thinking about the kiss *they'd* shared or imagining the one Will gave her tonight?

"I guess you and Will hit it off," he said.

"Your brother's very nice."

"What did you talk about?"

She yawned. "It's late, Conway, and I'm beat."

He grabbed his keys off the kitchen table. "I'll see you Monday."

"Conway?"

He stopped at the door and faced her.

"Thank you for setting up the date with Will." She smiled. "He was a big improvement over yucky Sean." She waited for Conway to speak but he remained silent, his brown eyes glowing with an emotion she couldn't identify.

Then he was gone. She crossed the room and flipped the lock on the door then thought about the twists and turns her relationship with Conway had taken the past couple of months. If anything good had come out of her date with Will, it was that they'd become friends. Once Conway found "the one" and moved on from her life for good and she'd need all the friends she could get to fill the hole he left behind.

THE THIRD WEEK of November had ushered in a dip in temperatures, nature's way of signaling the beginning of the pecan harvest. Conway stood at the edge of the grove, deciding how best to collect the nuts.

"Getting ready to start up the shaker machine?"

Startled, Conway spun and came face-to-face with Will. "I thought you were at a job site with Ben."

"We finished early." Will held out a key.

"What's that for?" Conway asked.

"Isi's trailer."

Isi had given Will an extra house key? "You're moving awfully fast with Isi, aren't you?" That his brother was spending time at the trailer when Conway wasn't there rubbed him every which way but right.

"I stopped by her place this afternoon to fix the window over her bed."

Will had gone into Isi's bedroom? Hell, Conway had yet to venture inside her private quarters. "Was Isi there?"

"Why all the questions?"

Conway wanted to wipe the smirk off his brother's face but refrained from throwing a punch. Isi would have a fit if he picked a fight in front of the twins. "I hope you know that Isi's not ready for anything serious."

"That's funny," Will said. "She told me she thought the boys needed a male role model in their lives."

Frustrated, Conway walked over to the shaker machine and adjusted the settings.

Will followed him. "You surprised Johnny."

Grateful for the change in subject, Conway asked, "How's that?"

"Johnny wasn't sure you meant it when you said you wanted to take over the farm."

If the eldest Cash brother had doubts, why hadn't he said anything to Conway? "I wouldn't have volunteered if I didn't intend to follow through."

"Grandpa would be proud of you."

Yeah, he would. "He loved his pecan trees."

"It was a good place to grow up, wasn't it?" Will

said. "Plenty of room to run without disturbing any neighbors."

"That's for sure."

Will pointed to the farmhouse, where Javier and Miguel played. "What do the boys do while you work in the orchards?"

"I made them bring their crayons and coloring books and told them to stay on the porch." Conway didn't want the kids anywhere near the shaker machine when he drove it through the rows.

"I could take the boys into town for root beers at Vern's Drive-In," Will said.

No way was Will honing in on his charges. "They're fine right where they are."

"If you say so."

"I say so." Conway gritted his teeth, pissed off that his brother had riled him.

"Think I'll say hi to the boys." Will walked off and it was all Conway could do to not tackle him to the ground.

Will stopped at the porch steps and spoke to them. Miguel laughed at whatever Will had said and it irked Conway that his brother amused the twins—that was his job.

Conway marched toward the group determined to find out what was so dang funny. He climbed the steps then froze. The boys had colored a highway system of roads from one end of the porch to the other. What happened to coloring in their books?

Miguel made *vroom-vroom* sounds as he moved a toy car over a bridge.

"Pretty ingenious if you ask me," Will said.

Conway glared at his brother. "No one asked you."

"Can I have a ride on the tractor?" Javier set his car aside.

"Not now. I want both of you to stay on the porch. It's too dangerous to be in the groves with pecans flying everywhere."

"I don't care if I get hit by one," Javier said.

"I'll make a deal with you," Conway said. "I'll give you a ride on the tractor after I finish each row." He figured one row up and down would take thirty minutes. He hoped the boys had enough patience to wait an hour. "Deal?"

"Okay," Javier said.

"What if we get hungry?" Miguel asked.

"I could—"

"I'll take care of that right now," Conway said, cutting off Will. He marched inside the house and rummaged through the pantry and fridge then returned with a stash of food—boxes of cereal, bags of chips, cans of soda and water bottles. "Don't eat all of this at once."

"What if we have to use the bathroom?" Javier said.

Before Will had a chance to offer his services again, Conway said, "Don't you have somewhere to go?"

Will raised his hands and backed away. "See you later, guys."

Conway motioned for the boys to follow him. "I'll show you where the toilet is." They trailed Conway through the kitchen and up the stairs to the second floor. He opened the bathroom door and the boys poked their heads inside. "Make sure you flush the toilet and wash your hands, okay?"

"Okay," the twins echoed.

They returned outside and Conway issued one last warning. "Don't leave the porch."

"We know," Miguel said.

"I'll be back when it's your turn for a ride on the tractor." Conway skipped down the steps and walked to the orchard where Will waited. "What are you still doing here?"

"I forgot to tell you Johnny said he got a call a few days ago from an agricultural company."

"What company?"

"Bell Farms out of southern California. They want buy the orchard."

"Why didn't Johnny tell me?" Conway asked.

"I think he's waiting to see how you do with this year's harvest."

"Grandpa would spin in his grave if we sold the place," Conway said.

"Johnny wants to discuss selling at Thanksgiving and put it to a vote."

Conway deserved more say in the decision than a simple vote.

"Good luck this afternoon." Will got in his truck and drove off.

After Conway started the tractor he decided he was more determined than ever to show his siblings he could bring in the harvest by himself. He steered the tractor into the second row of trees, where the vibrating robotic arms shook trunk after trunk until it rained pecans.

After the fifteenth tree he noticed Miguel and Javier waving their arms at the end of the row. He turned off the tractor and shouted, "What's the matter?"

Miguel spoke but Conway was too far away to make out the words. He hopped off the machine and walked toward the boy. "What's wrong?"

"We don't want to color anymore," Miguel said.

Swallowing his irritation, Conway said, "You can watch TV in the bunkhouse." Isi had told him that she didn't allow the boys to watch TV very often, but he was running out of ideas to entertain them. Inside the bunkhouse he turned on the big-screen TV mounted against the wall across from the row of single beds. "What channel?" Will had installed a satellite dish behind the shed and they got over a hundred different television programs.

"Disney," Javier said.

While Conway flipped through the directory, he noticed Miguel studying the posters of rodeo cowboys above the beds. "Do you like rodeo?"

Miguel shrugged.

"Have you ever been to a rodeo?"

The boys shook their heads no. Shoot, Conway had competed in his first mutton bustin' contest when he'd turned five. He positioned the sofa toward the TV. "Sit down." After they crawled onto the cushions, he said, "Don't get into any trouble."

"Is it my turn for a ride?" Javier asked.

"Not yet." The way things were going Conway would be lucky to drive the shaker machine through five rows before dark. "I'll come get you in a while."

A half hour later, Conway had made it to the end of the row and was about to head down another when Miguel dashed across the yard. The kid couldn't sit still for a minute. He raced up the porch steps, gathered an armful of snacks and attempted to carry them to the bunkhouse. He made it halfway, before he lost his load.

Conway considered helping Miguel, but he didn't have time. An hour later he shut down the machine and went into the bunkhouse. "You guys ready for a ride?" He gaped at the table covered in candy wrappers. "Did you eat all Porter's candy?"

"He lets us eat his candy," Miguel said.

"You didn't ask him."

"Can we ask him when he gets back?" Javier said.

"Forget it. You want a ride on the tractor or not?" He hated losing his patience, but he'd yet to make decent progress and half the afternoon was gone. When they reached the tractor, Conway sat Miguel next to him on the seat and Javier in his lap. He wasn't wasting time giving separate rides.

When they pleaded for Conway to show them how the shaker machine worked, he gave in and allowed the twins to remain on the tractor as he drove down the row, shaking tree after tree. Javier appeared fascinated by the process, Miguel not so much—he grew antsy and wanted to get off the tractor. When Conway reached the end of the row, he sent the boys back to the bunkhouse with the promise to check on them in an hour.

Time flew by and Conway shut down the tractor and shaker machine and made his way through the orchard. He got to within fifteen yards of the bunkhouse and heard shouting.

"You're in big trouble!" Miguel's voice carried through an open window.

"No, I'm not, you are!" Javier said.

Conway opened the door and stepped inside.

Both boys looked at each other and said, "He did it."

Conway stared in disbelief at the large-screen TV resting facedown on the cement floor. "Don't move." He crossed the room, grasped both boys by the seat of their pants and lifted them away from the broken glass, then carried them outside. "What the heck were you doing in there?" He didn't give the boys a chance to answer. "That TV cost over a thousand dollars."

The boys' eyes widened.

He shoved a hand through his hair. "How am I supposed to harvest the pecans if you two won't stay out of trouble?"

"We didn't mean to break the TV," Miguel said.

"Stay here." Conway retrieved a broom and dust-pan from the storage closet then spent the next twenty minutes sweeping up glass. When he returned outside, the boys were lying on their backs in the dirt staring up at the sky.

"How much is a thousand dollars?" Miguel asked, crawling to his knees.

"A lot of money."

Miguel kicked Javier's leg. "It's your fault." Miguel faced Conway. "Javi threw his pillow at me, but I ducked and it hit the TV."

"Are you gonna be mad at us forever?" Javier asked, getting to his feet.

"No, but I need time to cool off." He walked the boys back to the porch.

"Are you gonna tell our mom we broke your TV?"

"I haven't decided." Conway's anger was dying a fast death at the scared expressions on the boys' faces. He'd broken his share of things as a kid and Grandma Ada hadn't punished him harshly.

"We're gonna be grounded forever." Miguel sighed.

The boys walked to the end of the porch and sat on the swing.

"We won't leave the porch," Javier said.

Conway trusted them to keep their word. No doubt they were more than a little worried about what their mother would say when she found out what they'd done.

Chapter Nine

Isi reread the first paragraph of her term paper, satisfied she'd nailed the opening. Three sentences later, her mind wandered. The boys should be awake by now. Rarely did they sleep in and she worried they were coming down with colds.

Last night when she'd arrived home from the bar, she'd been surprised to find Conway's truck parked in front of her trailer, because they'd agreed that the boys would sleep at the farm while he harvested the pecans. When she'd asked why he'd brought them home, he'd said he thought it was best that they sleep in their own beds.

She shut down the computer and left the kitchen. When she opened her sons' door, she discovered them dressed and sitting on their beds, wearing glum expressions. "Hey, you two, what's the big secret?" Their eyes widened—not a good sign.

"Aren't you hungry?" she asked.

They hopped off their beds and filed past her, shoes dragging across the carpet. *Oh, dear.* They sat at the kitchen table and she felt their foreheads—no fever. "What's going on?"

"Conway's mad at us," Miguel said.

"Why?" When neither of them explained, she pulled

out a chair and sat. "What happened at the farm yesterday?"

Javier refused to make eye contact with her, so she swung her gaze to Miguel. "I'm waiting…"

"We broke Conway's TV."

Isi gasped. "How?"

Miguel stamped his foot. "It was Javi's fault!"

"Was not!"

"Was so!"

"Stop." She slapped her hand against the table, startling her sons. "Javi, how did the TV break?"

"We had a pillow fight 'cause we were bored."

"Where was the TV?" she asked.

"In the bunkhouse," Miguel said.

Why had the boys been in the bunkhouse by themselves? Conway had promised to keep them close by while he worked.

"How big was the TV?" Isi mentally calculated the meager amount she'd saved for the boys' Christmas presents.

"This big." Javier spread his arms wide.

"It cost a thousand dollars," Miguel said.

A thousand dollars?

Why hadn't Conway told her about the TV last night?

Because he knows you don't have the money to replace it.

Isi rubbed her brow. Conway had done so much to help her—more than he should have, and the boys breaking his TV made her feel horrible. "We're going to have to pay for a new TV."

As she cooked breakfast, she worried over how she'd come up with the money to replace the TV. Maybe Conway would allow her to make monthly payments. Poor Conway—he needed a break from her sons. She could skip class but not work—she couldn't afford to lose any hours when she lived paycheck to paycheck. There had been many times when she'd almost given in and confronted Tyler Smith, demanding he pay child support but pride had stopped her. If she'd had to choose between her pride and feeding the boys she would have pursued Tyler with relentless determination, but things had never gotten that bad.

A half hour later Conway's truck pulled in front of the trailer and Isi's heart pounded with dread. "Conway's here." She turned from the window and caught her sons fleeing to their bedroom. *Chickens.*

She met a sober-faced Conway at the door. "The boys told me about the TV. I'm sorry."

He shrugged off her apology. "It was my fault. I shouldn't have left them alone in the bunkhouse."

"The boys knew better than to have a pillow fight when they were a guest in someone else's home." She squeezed his hand. "I want to cover the cost of the TV, but I'll have to make monthly payments."

"You're not paying for the TV," he said.

When the boys' bedroom door banged open, Isi realized she still held Conway's hand. She released her grip as her sons walked into the living room with their ceramic piggy banks.

"You can have our money to pay for a new TV." Miguel held out his pig to Conway.

"Mine, too," Javier said.

Isi was so proud of her sons.

"And you can smash 'em 'cause we smashed your TV," Miguel said.

"I have an idea on how you can make up for breaking the TV," Conway said.

"How?" Miguel asked.

"You're both going to collect the branches and twigs that fall from the trees after the shaker machine knocks the nuts loose."

"How many sticks do we gotta collect?" Javier asked.

"All of them." Conway kept a straight face, and Isi bit her lip to keep from laughing at her sons' astonished expressions.

"Let's get going. We've got a lot of work to do." Conway held open the door and waited for the boys to put their banks away.

"Be good." Isi watched them walk off as if marching to the gallows. Once they were out of earshot, she said, "Please let me make payments on the TV."

"Forget about it, Isi. It was an accident. Porter and Buck are shopping for a new TV right now." He stepped onto the porch. "See you tonight."

"You're bringing the boys back here to sleep then?"

"I think it's best for all three of us to have a break from each other at night."

"Would you mind staying a bit longer then? Will and I are going to a late movie at the mall after I get off work."

"You're going out with Will again?"

"You sound surprised," she said.

"Will never said anything to me."

"Is it okay if we go to the movies?"

"I guess."

He didn't sound too enthusiastic. Maybe Conway was jealous of his brother.

She could only hope.

"How come we gotta get boots?" Miguel asked, following Conway through Boot Barn with Javier.

"'Cause that's what rodeo cowboys wear. Jeans, a

long-sleeve shirt and boots." Conway had felt guilty the past week while he'd harvested the nuts. Since breaking the TV, the boys had been on their best behavior and hadn't stepped off the porch—not once—unless Conway said it was okay. He'd finished most of the harvesting and was ahead of schedule, that's why he decided to surprise the twins and take them to a rodeo, where they could enter a mutton bustin' competition.

"Can I help you, sir?" An older gentleman approached them.

"These wranglers need a pair of boots," Conway said.

"Have a seat." The salesman pulled up a bench. "Be right back." He brought two boot boxes from the storeroom and knelt before the twins. He slid a brown pair on Javier's feet and a black pair on Miguel's. "Walk in them and tell me if they fit."

The boys shuffled up and down the aisle.

"What do you think?" Conway asked.

"I want the black ones," Javier said.

"I want the brown ones," Miguel said.

The salesman shook his head. "Thought for sure I had the right colors picked out for them."

"Okay, switch boots," Conway said.

Once the boys traded pairs, they raced to the end of the aisle. "Can we wear 'em now?" Javier asked.

"You bet." The salesman placed the boys' sneakers into the boot boxes then escorted them to the register and Conway got out his credit card.

After they left the store, he drove to Somerton, a small town twelve miles south of Yuma, where the Tamale Festival was in full swing. The annual event was sponsored by an Arizona State University Alumni chapter and the proceeds benefited local students attending ASU. Mutton bustin' happened to be one of the moneymakers at the festival and Conway hoped the boys would have fun.

"Where are we going?" Miguel spoke from the back-seat.

"The Tamale Festival."

"My mom makes tamales," Javier said.

"What are we gonna do at the festival?"

Conway glanced at Miguel in the rearview mirror. The kid never stopped talking. "Wait and see." Fifteen minutes later, he parked in a gravel lot next to a small outdoor arena then opened the back door and helped the boys out of the truck. As soon as their boots hit the ground, Conway said, "Wait here." He rummaged through the truck toolbox and removed a pair of straw cowboy hats then set them on the twins' heads. "Now you're ready to rodeo."

After paying for their admission, he bought hot dogs then they sat in the stands and ate, while watching rodeo helpers set up the arena for the mutton bustin' contest.

"Ladies and gents, welcome to the twenty-first annual Tamale Festival and Rodeo. Hold on to your hats, we're about to kick off the mutton bustin' races." After the announcer spoke, one of the chute doors opened across the arena and a sheep ran out with a young boy clinging to its back.

Both Javier and Miguel watched the sheep race through the arena. The kid finally fell off then he got to his feet and waved to his parents in the stands.

"Well, folks, Billy Baker will have to keep working on his technique. Better luck next time, buckaroo!"

"What do you guys think? Would you like to ride a sheep?" Conway asked.

"Can we?" Miguel's eyes shone with excitement. Javier inched closer to Conway.

"You don't have to ride, Javi. Only if you want to."

Javi poked Miguel in the shoulder. "You go first."

"Let's sign you up, Miguel." Conway guided the boys through the throng of rodeo fans to a table next to the chutes. While they waited in line, he studied a man and his daughter a few feet ahead of them. The cowboy looked familiar. He turned and Conway recognized him. Tyler Smith's gaze clashed with Conway's then he spotted the twins and stiffened. Even though Isi had told Conway that Smith had rejected his sons, the cowboy had probably seen her and the boys around town.

"Smith," Conway said.

"Cash." There were questions in Smith's eyes, but damned if Conway would answer them. "Is your daughter entering the contest?"

"Yes." Smith's gaze strayed back to the boys.

"We gotta move up." Miguel tugged on Conway's hand.

"Hold on, Miguel," Conway said.

"Are you gonna ride a sheep?" Javier asked the young girl standing with Smith.

She smiled shyly and nodded.

"Me, too," Javier said.

Hell, the boys had no clue the little girl was their half sister. Talk about ironic—Tyler Smith's kids all chatting together as if they were best friends. Smith's face paled as he took his daughter's hand and pulled her out of line. "Let's go."

"But, Daddy…"

Conway didn't catch the rest of the girl's words as her father walked off with her.

"How come they left?" Javi asked.

"I don't think her father was feeling well." Served Smith right to see what he'd tossed aside. They moved up in line and Conway paid Miguel's entry fee then pinned his contestant number to the back of his shirt.

Next they stood behind the sheep chute, waiting their turn. The boys took in all the action, watching the rodeo helpers put helmets on the kids before setting them on the sheep.

"Ready, cowboy?" a rodeo worker asked when Miguel arrived at the front of the line. Once he sat on the sheep, Conway said, "Wait a second. I want to take a picture." He removed the camera he'd purchased at the drugstore earlier in the week after he'd decided to take the boys to the rodeo. Isi was always snapping photos of the boys, and he figured she'd be upset if she didn't have pictures of them mutton bustin'.

"Done," he said.

The gate opened and the sheep trotted into the arena.

He climbed the rails to take a second picture. "Go get 'em, Miguel!"

Miguel had no trouble hanging on until the sheep switched gears and ran hard. Conway thought for sure the boy would fall, but he clung to the sheep's fur. The cheering crowd rose to their feet.

Hang on, Mig. Hang on, buddy.

Miguel made it all the way across the arena before the rodeo helpers caught up with the sheep and cornered it.

"Folks, I think you witnessed a future National Finals Rodeo bronc rider!"

As applause echoed through the stands, Conway felt Smith's eyes watching him from two chutes away. He'd thought the man had left the rodeo. Pissed off, Conway hopped down from the rails. "Stay here, Javi. I'll be right back."

He approached Smith. "You're an ass, you know that? And wipe that grin off your face. You haven't earned the right to smile at your son." Conway didn't know what had possessed him to speak that like to Smith, but he felt protective of the boys.

"This is none of your business, Cash."

"The hell you say?" Conway noticed a woman talking to the little girl Smith had been with at the sign-in table—probably his wife. "You're wrong. It is my business, you know why?" Smith didn't rise to the bait. "You abandoned your sons. I know all about fathers who walk out on their kids. Those kids never want anything to do with their fathers after they're grown-up. When you're old and wanting to make amends for your sins, don't expect forgiveness." He nodded to Javier and Miguel back at the sheep chute. "Kids don't forget and they don't forgive." He'd had his say, so Conway walked off.

"Are you mad, Conway?" Javi asked.

"No. You did great, Miguel. I'm proud of you." He gave the boy a high five.

"Javi you gotta try it," Miguel said.

Conway bent down and looked Javier in the eye. "You ready?"

Javier slipped his hand inside Conway's. "What if I get hurt?"

"You won't, 'cause you gotta wear a helmet," Miguel said. "C'mon, Javi, you can do it."

Javier straightened his shoulders. "I'm gonna ride."

Once Conway paid his entry fee, the rodeo helpers put a helmet on Javier and set him on the sheep's back. The gate opened and Conway snapped two pictures before Javi slipped sideways and dropped to the ground. He got up, brushed off his jeans and raced back to the chute.

Out of breath Javier said, "Can I do that again?"

"Sure." Whether Isi knew it or not, her sons were rodeo cowboys in the making and Conway couldn't be prouder of them.

Isi WAVED AS she watched Will drive out of the trailer park. They'd skipped stopping for dessert after the movie. Will insisted Conway wouldn't mind, but Isi hadn't wanted to take advantage of her sitter by staying out too late. When she stepped inside the trailer, she spotted Conway asleep on the couch. She treaded closer to the sofa. He was such a handsome man. If only...

"I'm a light sleeper, if you're thinking about pulling a prank on me." He opened his eyes.

Isi lost herself in his warm gaze.

"Where's Will?" Conway sat up.

"He left." She shrugged out of her jacket. "How did the boys behave?"

"Fine. We played hooky." He stretched his arms above his head, drawing her gaze to his chest.

"You didn't work at the farm?" she asked.

"We drove over to Somerton for the Tamale Festival."

Isi had always wanted to attend the festival. "Did you rodeo?"

"Nope, but the boys entered the mutton bustin' competition."

"Really?" She'd heard about the event for kids. "Javier rode, too?"

"He was nervous, but after watching Miguel he wanted to give it a try." Conway grinned.

"What?"

"Miguel rode his sheep 'til the buzzer and won a blue ribbon."

Isi smiled. That sounded like her competitive son. "How did Javier do?"

"He fell off after a few seconds. Miguel said he'd share his ribbon with him."

"Did you by chance take any pictures?"

Conway went into the kitchen then returned with a photo envelope from a local drugstore.

Isi browsed through the pictures. "These are great," she said. "Where did they get the boots?"

"We stopped at Boot Barn on the way out of town."

"You shouldn't have spent money on them," she said. She'd be indebted to Conway for life if he continued to buy things for the boys. As it was, she doubted she'd be able to pay for the bunkhouse TV until she landed a new job after she graduated. "Thank you for taking the photos."

"So you and Will are really hitting it off," he said.

"Will's a nice guy." She noticed his frown and asked, "What's wrong?"

"Will's too old for you."

"He's not that much older than you."

"Maybe not, but if you two get serious, I—"

"Right now we're friends, Conway."

"That could change, but my brother's not the right man for the twins."

"You can't be serious."

"Hey, I've been with the boys long enough to know who would make a good dad for them."

"Oh, really?" *This ought to be interesting.* "What kind of man do you think the boys need in their life?"

Conway shoved a hand through his hair and paced across the room. "They need a man who won't get upset when they make a mess with their toys."

Like you. "Go on."

"A guy, who doesn't mind being interrupted and asked a million questions."

Like you.

"A guy who'll teach them to stand up for themselves."

Like you did.

"A man who'll appreciate their differences and not compare one to the other."

Oh, Conway, can't you see you're describing yourself? "If Will's not the right man for me and the boys then who is?"

Was it a trick of the light or had Conway's eyes sparked at her question?

"I don't know, but it's not my brother." He closed the distance between them and Isi felt the air squeeze out of the room. He stared into her eyes, the sexy tilt of his mouth making her heart race. Would it always be like this between them—his brown eyes making her knees go weak?

"Isi?" he whispered, drawing her gaze to his lips.

"What?" She couldn't think with Conway standing so close.

The next thing she knew, Conway's breath fanned her cheek and her skin broke out in goose bumps.

"Tell me what kind of guy rocks your world and I'll find him for you."

She held her breath. He stood so close all she had to do was lift her face and her mouth would brush his jaw. "You'll never find him."

"Why not?"

Because he's standing right here in front of me, and he doesn't want to be found.

She swayed forward, bringing their mouths closer. *Kiss me, Conway.*

He must have heard her silent plea. His lips brushed across hers and her body tingled as if he were running his hand over her naked flesh. He pulled back, his gaze piercing. "This isn't a good idea." He didn't allow her a chance to speak before he kissed her again, this time, his mouth lingering.

"Tell me to stop." His dark eyes gleamed. He wanted her, but he couldn't promise her anything more than this night in his arms.

Is one night enough?

Isi had dreamed of making love to Conway for weeks. She hadn't had sex since the boys were born and to end a four-year drought in Conway's arms was nothing short of a dream come true. But once she got a taste of his passion, would she be able to distance herself from the experience and return to being his friend and confidante?

She caressed his scruffy cheek, relishing the prickly feel of his five-o'clock shadow. The yearning to be intimate with him overpowered her common sense.

Standing on tiptoe, she whispered, "I don't want to stop you."

He grasped her face, sweeping his tongue inside her mouth, leaving no doubt in her mind what he wanted.

Her.

Chapter Ten

Like a drunken cowboy, Conway stumbled after Isi through the hallway. As soon as he entered her bedroom, she shut the door and flipped the lock. The light from the street lamps behind the trailer park flooded the room, casting Isi in a mystic glow.

Not a hint of doubt showed in her beautiful brown eyes. When she ran her tongue across her lower lip, leaving a moist trail on the pouting flesh, Conway's testosterone level went through the roof.

There was no doubt Isi wanted him. Her fingers moved with confidence over the buttons of her blouse until the sides fell open revealing the creamy swells of her breasts above her black lace bra.

"You next," she said.

So that's how they were playing this game. He ripped open the snaps on his shirt, baring his chest. She flashed a wicked smile that jolted his heart. She unbuckled her belt then slid the zipper down on her jeans. A bit of black lace peeked at him and Conway scrambled to undo his belt and release the buttons on his fly.

"I guess we both prefer black undergarments," she said, staring at his briefs.

Conway shrugged out of his shirt then closed the distance between them. He brushed her blouse aside, exposing her shoulder then he kissed her skin. The scent of perfume and warm female made him crazy hungry for her.

"You're beautiful." He cupped her small breast and kissed the nipple through the lace. Her moan echoed in his ears, and when her hand found his arousal, he knew he wouldn't last long. He lifted her into his arms and carried her to the bed. He kissed her once, twice, three times before coming up for air. "How do you want this? Hard and fast or slow and easy?"

"Let's save the slow and easy for next time."

"I was hoping you'd say that." He reached for his jeans on the floor, but Isi intercepted his arm. "I've got it covered." She rummaged through her nightstand drawer and held out a new box of condoms. "After getting pregnant with the twins, I don't want to be caught unprepared again."

"Are you sure?"

"I've never been so sure of anything."

He slid her panties off then sheathed himself and thrust inside her, groaning in pleasure. Everything about Isi and this moment felt right. Perfect. His fingers coaxed her to keep pace with him and when he heard the quiet hitch in her breath followed by her muffled cry against his chest, he let himself go, and followed her to paradise.

SOFT GUTTURAL SNORES and the hot press of naked flesh dragged Isi from slumber. Conway spooned her body, one arm stretching beneath her pillow and the other resting along her thigh.

Conway's chest pushed against her shoulders when he inhaled, then a sliver of cool air rushed between their bodies when he exhaled. The hair on his thighs tickled her bottom, but it was the rhythmic puff of air hitting the back her neck that made her skin break out in goose pimples.

The muffled wail of a police siren echoed in the distance, reminding her of the stark contrast between their childhoods—Conway having been raised on a pecan farm in the country and Isi having grown up in the poorest barrio in Buenos Aires. How different her life would be right now if her father had been a farmer and not a factory worker.

Isi didn't often allow herself to think too far into the future, beyond earning her degree and landing a stable job—mostly because of fear. Fear that another roadblock would prevent her from graduating. Fear that she'd never find a job that made enough money to move her and the boys out of the trailer and into a real home. Fear that her sons would grow up without a father.

Fear that she'd spend the rest of her life alone.

In Conway's arms, she felt safe enough to dream. She imagined waking in the mornings on the farm, hearing the boys arguing down the hall in their bedroom. She envisioned cooking a country breakfast before walking her sons to the meet the bus. When the boys returned from school, they'd jump on the tractor and help Conway in the pecan groves.

But happy ever after on a farm would never be a reality, because Conway didn't want to be a father.

No matter how much Isi wished otherwise, she'd known from the get-go that raising children was not in his future. She'd experienced plenty of disappointment in her young life—more than most women her age. No matter what happened between her and Conway, she'd survive, because she had her sons. Javier and Miguel were her greatest joy. Her purpose in life. Her reason for living.

Forcing her thoughts from the boys and the future, she basked in the glow of Conway's lovemaking. If Isi had learned one thing after their conversations about women, it was that Conway needed to be a priority in his lady's life. He wanted to be the center of her world, but when their clothes had come off, he'd focused on her pleasure, not his.

He'd been amazing in bed. Of course, she'd only had two lovers to compare him with—her high school boyfriend and the twins' father. Neither had come near to the passion she'd found in Conway's arms. She doubted she'd ever close her eyes without hearing his deep voice murmur how much he adored her body. He'd made her feel young, sexy and carefree and for a short time she'd forgotten she was a mother, student and waitress. She glanced at the nightstand clock.

If only time would stand still.

If only she, Conway and the boys were a real family.

If only Conway would wake up and ask her to marry him.

Wishful thinking.

Of course he wouldn't propose, but what if they could be friends with benefits until "the one" happened along?

What about Javi and Mig?

There were times she hated the voice inside her head, always challenging her decisions. Even if she hid her affair with Conway so the boys wouldn't get their hopes up that he'd become their dad, would she be able to stop herself from falling in love with him?

If there was one thing she'd learned about herself the past few years, it was that she was a survivor. When

Conway found his perfect woman, she'd pick up the pieces of her broken heart and move on.

He stretched behind her, his hand moving over her breast, caressing her. Then she felt the press of his mouth on the top of her head.

She turned in his arms and he spread tiny kisses over her face, drawing sighs and moans from her before he sheathed himself and took her on another fantasy ride.

When their breathing returned to normal, he whispered, "You're amazing."

His smile melted her heart. "So are you."

"It's almost five." He squinted at the bedside clock. "I'm usually out in the barn by now."

The sun wouldn't be up for two hours. They had time… "Stay." She squeezed his bicep. "You work too hard."

"Not as hard as you." Conway kissed her forehead. "I don't know how you do it, taking care of the twins, going to college, working at the bar then studying when you get home." He slid down on the mattress and nuzzled her breasts.

"I want you to know…"

Conway stiffened. He'd woken up in enough beds with pink-flowered sheets to have learned that most morning-after conversations didn't bode well for him.

"That last night was special," she said.

He couldn't concentrate when she toyed with his nipple. "Isi…we can't do this again."

Her eyes widened and he felt like an ass. He'd shared an incredible few hours with Isi, which had been way better than any fantasy he'd had about her the past two years. The least he could do is wait until they had their clothes on to discuss whether or not there would be a repeat of tonight in the future.

He didn't want to be the bad guy, but there was no way he'd take advantage of Isi and keep carrying on with her when he had no intention of making their relationship permanent.

"I'm not going to change how I feel about being a father," he said. "You deserve to be with a man who'll make your sons a priority in his life. I'm not that man."

She raked her fingernails down his back and he shivered. "We could be friends with benefits."

Was she saying what he thought she was saying? A creaking sound in the hall startled Isi and she flew off the bed, dragging the sheet with her.

"Oh, my God!" She motioned to the window above the bed as she backed against the door. "Get out!" she whispered.

He shoved his legs into his jeans then stuffed his bare feet into his boots, wincing at the tight fit.

"Mom? My throat hurts."

When the door handle jiggled, Isi gestured frantically.

"Mom?"

"Be right there, Miguel."

Conway yanked the blinds up and opened the window, then punched out the screen with his fist. "Sorry," he mumbled as he stepped on her sheets and launched himself out the window. When his boots hit the ground, he poked his head through the window. "My keys."

Isi tossed his keys and wallet. He caught them then raced bare-chested to his truck.

It wasn't until he reached the city limits that he caught himself smiling in the rearview mirror. Good thing Will had fixed Isi's sticky window or he would have had to explain to Miguel what he'd been doing in his mother's bedroom.

"Look who came crawling home before dawn?"

Conway froze when he stepped from his truck and heard Porter's voice echo in the darkness.

"Over here." Porter sat up in the bed of his truck.

"What are you doing?" Conway asked.

"I couldn't sleep."

Couldn't sleep? "Twenty-seven is too young to be suffering from insomnia."

"Not being able to sleep has nothing to do with my melatonin levels and everything to do with Betsy."

Although he'd earned a reputation of being a ladies' man, Porter never lacked for female attention. And while Conway was on a mission to find the right woman to settle down with, his brother played the dating game for the sake of competing, not caring in the end if he lost or won.

Of all the brothers, Conway and Porter resembled each other the most in appearance, but they couldn't be more different. Porter was a goof-off, who took life one day at a time. Conway liked having fun as much as the next guy, but the past couple of years he'd been thinking there was more to life.

"Where's your shirt?" Porter's white teeth flashed in the predawn light.

If given a choice Porter was not the brother he'd have picked to have a serious conversation with, but Conway was rattled by what he and Isi had done and he needed to vent. "I crossed the line with a woman I shouldn't have."

"What happened?"

"I slept with Isi."

"The twins' mother?"

What other Isi was there?

"She's single," Porter said. "What's the problem?"

"I have no intention of marrying her, so we shouldn't have slept together."

"I have no intention of marrying Betsy, but I still slept with her."

"Who's Betsy?"

"Betsy Brumfield. We met at Vern's Drive-In a few days ago and hit it off."

"That was quick."

"Betsy invited me back to her apartment after the movie." Porter shrugged. "I wasn't going to say no."

"Do you ever think about settling down with one woman?"

Porter waved a hand in the air. "Quit talking about me. Why are you upset about sleeping with Isi? Does she already have a steady boyfriend?"

"No!" Conway shoved a hand through his hair. "But I let my emotions get the best of me. I was frustrated."

"By what?"

He didn't want Porter to know he was jealous of Will. "Isi went out on a date with a guy and the whole night I worried that she was having sex with him."

"If you don't like the idea of Isi dating, then you must have feelings for her."

"We've been friends for a long time."

"How come you've never invited her to spend a holiday with us?" Porter asked.

"Because we're not that kind of friends."

Porter stared at him with a perplexed frown. "What the hell kind of friends are you?"

When had his younger brother become so pushy? "I stop by the Border Town Bar & Grill a few times a week and we talk."

"Ah."

Conway quirked an eyebrow. "Ah, what?"

"Isi's your therapist."

Not only was Porter pushy, he was perceptive, too.

"Let me see if I have this figured out." Porter sat up straight. "You and Isi are friends and she listens to all your problems, offers advice and basically keeps you focused on your goals, whatever those are."

"Right."

"So the reason you're all worked up over having sex with her is that you're afraid she won't view you as a friend anymore and you won't be able to bend her ear like you used to."

"Not at all. I—"

"Wait," Porter interrupted. "You're afraid that if Isi becomes involved with a guy, then he'll put the brakes on your friendship with her."

"No." Conway's anxiety had nothing to do with being cut off from Isi's counsel—did it? He'd grown close to her and the boys these past weeks, and accepted that he couldn't have her and the twins for himself but that didn't mean he wanted some other guy to have them.

"If you value Isi's friendship that much, why did you sleep with her?" Porter asked.

"When she walked in the door, all I could think about was kissing her and—"

"Staking your claim on her."

Had he wanted to stake his claim on Isi? "She didn't try to stop me when I kissed her."

"I have that problem all the time," Porter said. "I usually hesitate right before I kiss a girl in case she changes her mind, then I—"

"Hey, back to my sex life, not yours."

"Sorry."

Agitated, Conway paced. "Making love with Isi was off-the-charts amazing." After they'd made love the first time, Isi had fallen asleep for a few minutes, giving Conway a chance to study her without her knowing. The sight of her pretty face relaxed and her breathing even and quiet had moved something deep inside him. His chest had swelled with tenderness and he'd felt connected to her in a way he'd never experienced with another woman. The intensity of that emotion had scared him but at the same time it had felt exhilarating.

"And good sex is a bad thing?"

"I can't have serious feelings for Isi because of her sons."

"What's wrong with Miguel and Javier? Aren't they good boys?"

"I don't want to be a father, Porter." He felt protective of the twins and he'd do everything possible to make sure they didn't get hurt, which meant he could never be their dad.

"Is it because the twins aren't yours?"

The fact that Conway hadn't fathered the twins had nothing to do with not wanting to be their father. He feared that if he continued sleeping with Isi, it would only be a matter of time before his feelings for her developed into love. The boys were a part of Isi—if he fell in love with her, how could he not love her sons?

"I like the twins fine, but I don't want the responsibility of raising them." That sounded better than telling his brother the truth—that he didn't trust himself not to cut out on Isi down the road—he was his father's son after all and abandoning women and children was in his DNA. What if he and Isi married and the boys accepted him as their father then six months later, the pressure of all that responsibility got to him and he split? Isi had already lost too many people she loved—he didn't want to be one more.

"A lot of guys can't envision themselves as fathers until their girlfriend or wife becomes pregnant. It happened to Gavin," Porter said. "He panicked when Dixie turned up pregnant. Now, he's a natural at taking care of Nathan."

Gavin was a better man than Conway. After the things his brother-in-law had witnessed in the army and the nightmares that had followed him home from the war in Afghanistan, it astonished Conway that Gavin always put Dixie and their son first in his life.

"Not wanting kids has nothing to do with a lack of confidence in my ability to be a father." Conway scuffed the toe of his boot on the ground. "I want to keep my life simple. Me and my wife. No kids." He was already taking a huge risk by committing to a woman he wasn't sure he could stay with a year much less a lifetime. "Lots of married couples choose not to have kids."

"True, but you grew up with five brothers and a sister," Porter said. "Won't the quiet drive you nuts?"

"Maybe."

"So what are you gonna do about Isi?"

"I'm for sure not going to have sex with her again." After she suggested friends with benefits, abstinence might prove challenging. He'd have to avoid being alone with her. "She'll understand. She knows I don't want kids."

"What if she doesn't care that you don't want kids and she's only in it for the sex?"

Conway gaped. Had his brother been spying on him and Isi from inside her bedroom closet?

"I guess the only problem with sleeping together—" Porter stretched his arms above his head and yawned "—is that sex would interfere with Isi trying to find a potential husband and you the perfect wife."

Exactly. Isi might want a brief affair until she finished her degree, but they'd been lucky they hadn't been discovered by the twins. Once she graduated, he'd have to end their friendship for good.

"Are Isi and the boys coming for Thanksgiving this Thursday?"

"Yeah, Dixie invited them," Conway said, unwilling to admit it had been Will's idea.

The sky glowed pink as the sun rose higher. "I better get to work," Conway said. "I have to watch the boys again on Monday and I need to get the orchard cleaned up this weekend."

"If you want, I can drive into Yuma and get the twins Monday morning."

"No rodeos?"

Porter shook his head. "I told Betsy I'd hang out with her this week."

"Where does she work?"

"The Pancake House in Yuma."

His brother was seeing a waitress, too. What was it about waitresses that attracted the Cash brothers? "If you're sincere about picking up the twins, I accept your offer."

"What time should I be at Isi's?" Porter asked.

"Eleven-thirty. I'll leave directions to the mobile-home park in the bunkhouse."

"Think I'll go to bed now and dream about Betsy." Porter hopped down from the truck.

Conway watched his brother walk off, thinking he didn't need sleep to dream about Isi—he could do it standing up with his eyes wide open.

"CONWAY'S HERE!" MIGUEL raced to the front door after hearing the bell ring.

Isi drew in a deep breath and exhaled slowly. Two days had passed since Conway escaped her trailer through the bedroom window and she'd been a wreck, waiting for his call or text. She'd received neither, which had only added to her anxiety.

She zipped her makeup bag and stowed it in the bathroom drawer then studied her reflection in the mirror. She looked the same, but she felt different—when she thought of Conway, her body tingled in places it had never tingled before.

Unsure how Conway would react after they'd crossed the friendship line, she left the bathroom then stopped dead in her tracks.

"Hey, you're not Conway." Miguel flashed a smile.

"Hi, Porter." Javier joined his brother at the door. "Did you eat all your Halloween candy?"

Porter stepped inside the trailer. "I think you guys ate all my candy."

When he looked Isi's way she said, "Hello, Porter." Worried Conway had been hurt at the farm, she asked, "Is Conway okay?"

"He's out in the orchard on the tractor right now."

Had Conway sent his brother to get the boys because he hadn't wanted to face her after they'd had sex? She tried not to read too much into the situation but couldn't help wondering if he regretted sleeping with her. The thought hurt more than she cared to admit.

"I'm not rodeoing this week," Porter said. "So I volunteered to fetch the troublemakers."

"We're not troublemakers. Are we, Mom?" Miguel asked.

"That's up for debate."

"What's a debate?" Javier asked.

"A big dispute," Porter answered.

"What's a dispute?" Miguel asked.

"A fight." Porter raised his arms and curled his hands into fists then punched the air above their heads. "It's a winner-take-all, knockout brawl."

The boys giggled and joined in the fun, swinging their arms at Porter as he dodged out of the way. Clutching her car keys Isi said, "Would you tell Conway I won't need his help during the day the rest of the week? I don't have classes again until after the holiday."

"Sure." Porter slapped a hand against his thigh. "I almost forgot to tell you. Dixie says we're eating at one o'clock Thanksgiving Day and not to worry about bringing anything."

Suddenly Isi wasn't so sure she should attend the Cash Thanksgiving celebration. What if Conway didn't want her there but couldn't say so without hurting the boys' feelings? Darn it. Why did morning-afters—make that two-day-afters—have to be so difficult?

"Tell Dixie I'd planned to make my mother's chorizo stuffing. It's spicy, but I think everyone will like it."

"Sounds great. Okay, guys, let's go. I've got to get ready for my hot date with Betsy." Porter ushered the boys out of the trailer and Isi locked the door behind everyone then handed the booster seats to Porter.

"Who's Betsy?" Miguel asked.

"A girl."

"What's a hot date?" Javier trailed after Porter and Miguel.

"Um…" Porter grinned over his shoulder at Isi. "A hot date is when you do lots of fun stuff."

The devilish gleam in Porter's eye gave Isi pause. Had Conway told his brother they'd had sex? *No.* Conway wasn't a sleep-and-tell kind of guy.

"What fun stuff?" Miguel moved out of the way while Porter installed the child seats.

"You know," Porter said. "Play with new toys and go fun places."

Javier climbed into his chair. "What fun places?"

"You two always ask this many questions?" Porter shut the door on the twins in the middle of their answer. He waved to Isi. "Don't worry. They won't hear any sex talk from me. Promise."

Porter's comment had Isi wondering all over again if Conway had confided in his brother about his relationship with her. Blushing she slid behind the wheel of her car and drove off. She'd have to wait until tonight to find out if sleeping with Conway had been the biggest mistake of her life.

Chapter Eleven

Conway had put the boys to bed a few minutes ago, but they'd yet to settle down. He sat on the sofa then reached for the remote and turned on the TV. A few minutes later the twins marched into the living room.

"What's wrong?" Conway asked, noting the brothers had put on their rodeo boots, only they must have done it in the dark, because they each wore one black boot and one brown boot.

"Here." Javier shoved a piece of paper at Conway.

He scanned the note. "This is your Christmas wish list."

Miguel shook his head. "We don't want 'em anymore."

"Why not?" He hoped Isi hadn't already purchased the toys.

"'Cause," Miguel said.

"Okay. What do you two want then?" Conway asked.

"We want you to be our dad," Javi said.

If Conway hadn't already been sitting down, his legs would have folded beneath him. The boys stared wide-eyed, waiting for his response. When he opened his mouth to speak, the words stuck to the sides of his throat. He swallowed hard, ignoring the panic building inside him. "I'm flattered, guys, but—"

"What's flattered?" Miguel asked.

"It means I appreciate you wanting me to be your father, but I can't."

"Why not?" Javi inched closer and set his small hand on Conway's thigh. "Don't you like us?"

"Of course I like you." Conway squeezed his hands into fists to keep from hugging the boy. How the heck did he get himself out of this mess without hurting their feelings? "I've had a lot of fun hanging out with both of you."

"You could be our dad and have fun with us all the time," Mig said.

Feeling like a cornered rabbit, Conway sprang from the couch and walked to the opposite side of the room then faced the boys. How could two kids three feet tall be so intimidating? "You guys don't understand. I'm not going to be anybody's father. Ever."

"Why not?" Javi asked.

"Because—" He shut his mouth. He couldn't very well tell them that if he became their father, odds were one day he'd wake up and walk out on them. "Don't worry, guys. Your mom will meet a really great man one day and he'll be your father."

"But we want you," Miguel said.

Feeling lower than pond scum, he said, "Get back in bed."

The twins didn't move and Conway feared they were going to defy him, then Miguel huffed and walked off.

Javier stood his ground and pointed to his mismatched boots. "You lied."

"About what?" Then Conway remembered telling the boy not to wear mismatched shoes all the time because the good luck would wear off. "I'm sorry, Javi."

The kid walked back to his bedroom and slammed

the door hard, shaking not only the trailer walls but Conway's heart. He'd handled the situation badly—more proof that being a father wasn't in the cards for him.

He waited an hour before opening the bedroom door and peeking in on the twins. They were asleep in their beds—thank goodness. He wouldn't have been able to stand it if he'd found them crying. As he closed the door his gaze landed on the garbage can across the room. They'd thrown both pairs of cowboy boots in the trash.

Feeling like the cruelest man on earth, Conway closed the door and returned to the living room. He had no idea what he was going to say to Isi when she got home tonight. They'd yet to talk about making love and now the boys had asked him to be their father.

Conway had been given a reprieve when Porter had volunteered to fetch the twins earlier in the day, but there was no escaping a face-off with Isi tonight. He still hadn't wrapped his head around the fact that he'd had sex with a woman who'd been his friend and confidante the past twenty-four months.

Every once in a while his thoughts of Isi would stray into X-rated territory when he remembered the past— like the night she'd worn a tight spandex top at the bar. When she'd caught him staring at her breasts, her nipples had hardened and it had taken all his willpower to act as if he hadn't noticed. Then there had been the night when she'd tripped over a bar stool and he'd caught her by the waist—except her waist had actually been her breast. He'd suffered erotic dreams for a month after that incident.

His attraction to Isi had always been there, simmering below the surface. If she hadn't had the boys, Conway would have fallen hard for her within the first week of meeting her.

He wanted to wipe the slate clean between them and return to the way things used to be—before he'd offered to babysit for the boys. He yearned for the days when he stopped by the bar and shared his latest dating dilemma with her and she'd make sense of it all for him. Now Isi was his dating dilemma, and he sure in heck couldn't her ask for advice on how to deal with *her*.

At twelve-thirty he heard Isi's clunker park beneath the carport. When she entered the trailer, their gazes clashed and his first thought was how hot she looked in her bar T-shirt and tight jeans. A surge of testosterone flooded his bloodstream as his mind flashed back to their clothes flying off in her bedroom.

"How was your day?" he asked.

"Fine." She set her backpack on the floor. "How about yours?"

"Fine," he lied. He swore he saw wavy tension lines hovering in the air between them.

"Conway."

"Isi."

They spoke simultaneously. "Ladies first," he said.

"That's okay. You go."

"About the other night." Damn, why was it so hard to tell her that making love with her again was never going to happen? "I don't think we should…you know…have a repeat of…" *Oh, hell.* For a guy who had a reputation of being a ladies' man, he sounded like an idiot. "It's not that I didn't enjoy what we did," he said. "It's that I don't want kids and—"

"I have the boys."

And tonight he'd discovered how much power kids wielded over adults and how they could make a grown man feel like crap.

"It's okay." Her sad smile tugged his heartstrings.

"I didn't invite you into my bed, hoping you'd change the way you feel about kids." She strolled past him into the kitchen and he caught a whiff of her perfume—the same stuff she'd worn the night they'd slept together. She drank a glass of water then set the cup in the sink. "I'm fine with keeping things between us casual until I graduate at the end of the semester and we go our separate ways."

Two very good reasons why he couldn't keep things casual with Isi were sleeping a few feet away behind a closed door. Heck, it was bad enough that he cared about the boys as if he were their…uncle or *something*. If he gave Isi half the chance, he'd begin caring for her like a steady boyfriend or… He couldn't make himself say the word *husband* out loud much less in his head.

"Porter said you don't have classes the rest of the week."

"That's right."

"I think it would be best if you found a new sitter to watch the boys when you go to work."

Isi's eyes widened then she dropped her gaze. Conway backed up a step to keep from taking her in his arms and begging for her forgiveness.

He edged toward the door, his stomach dropping when he caught her wiping a tear.

She sniffed. "Conway?"

"Yeah?"

"Would it be better if the boys and I don't show up at the farm for Thanksgiving?"

He'd forgotten Will had invited them. "You should still come."

"Are you sure?"

"Positive." *Leave. Don't stay no matter how badly she acts like she needs a hug.* Conway closed the door behind him and jogged to his truck. When he started the engine it occurred to him that his actions tonight proved he was no better than his own father—for all intents and purposes he'd turned his back on Isi and the boys. Better that he found out now rather than later after all their hearts became entangled.

As soon as Conway's truck pulled away from the trailer, Isi broke down in tears and swiped angrily at the moisture that leaked from her eyes. What an idiot she'd been to believe that if Conway made love to her once he'd want to share her bed again.

Suck it up, girl.

Conway had done so much for her and the boys that she refused to make him feel guilty for not wanting to carry on an affair with her. She hated to be the one to break the news to her sons, but first thing in the morning she'd continue her search for a new sitter. If she didn't have any luck, she'd beg her neighbor for help. Mrs. Sneed might not be as exciting as Conway but at least she wasn't a pedophile or a crazy lady.

After turning out the lights, she stopped in the hallway and poked her head inside the boys' bedroom. Javier was wide awake. "What's the matter, honey? Did you have a nightmare?" She sat on the bed, pulled him into her arms and rocked him.

"Conway doesn't want to be our dad," he said.

Isi stiffened. What was Javi talking about?

"I asked him to be our dad for Christmas instead of getting presents from Santa, but he said no."

So it wasn't sleeping with her that had scared Conway off. "When did you ask him?"

"Tonight."

When Isi turned her head away so Javier wouldn'

see her tears, she noticed the trash can. "Why did you throw your boots in the garbage?"

"They're bad luck."

She had no idea what Javi was talking about, but she didn't want to ask for an explanation. "Honey, Conway is a nice man and he really likes you and Mig, but he never planned to be with us forever." She didn't know how to explain Conway's fear of fatherhood when *she* didn't fully understand his reasons for not wanting children.

"We don't want Conway to watch us anymore."

You're getting your wish. "Tomorrow we'll find a new sitter."

Miguel lay wide awake staring at her. She waited for him to say what was on his mind, but he kept silent. "You okay, Mig?"

He rolled away and flung the covers over his head. His heart was broken, too. She gave Javi an extra hug then tucked in his blankets. "We have each other, guys. The three of us will always be a family."

She left the door cracked open before retreating to her bedroom where she changed into her pajamas and slipped into bed.

Then she cried, her sobs muffled by the pillow pressed against her face.

Isi DRIED THE last of the Thanksgiving dishes and set the damp towel on the counter. She'd volunteered to help Dixie in the kitchen so she could escape the awkwardness between her and Conway. Even the boys had chosen to stick by Will's side this afternoon—not that she blamed them.

"This is a lovely home, Dixie."

"The house is over a hundred years old and Will is

constantly repairing leaky faucets and creaky doors. The place needs a facelift, but no one has the time or money to update the rooms."

"I wouldn't change a thing." Isi strolled into the dining room off the kitchen. She studied the wallpaper pattern of elegantly intertwining white blooms against a faded burned-gold background. The space was cozy and inviting.

"Would you like a tour of the house?" Dixie asked.

Isi had been dying for such an invitation. "I'd love to see the other rooms."

"Let's start upstairs."

She followed Dixie out of the kitchen and asked, "Does Shannon want to come?"

"Shannon practically grew up in this house. She spent more time here than at her father's ranch." Dixie stopped by the front door and looked in the parlor. "I don't know where she disappeared to."

"Maybe she's outside." Those who weren't helping clean up after the meal were playing touch football in the yard.

"There are three bedrooms upstairs," Dixie said.

Isi stepped on a squeaky stair. "Are these the original wood floors?"

"Yep. They've taken a lot of abuse over the years and need to be refinished."

"I like the noise, it's charming."

"My grandparents never minded the loose boards, because they warned them when one of my brothers snuck into the house past curfew." Dixie stopped outside the door at the top of the stairs. "This is where Gavin and I sleep."

"Nice," Isi said.

"It's considered the master, but all three bedrooms

are the same size. The only difference is that this room has three windows, not two." Dixie opened the next door.

"Cowboy and Indian wallpaper."

"Believe it or not this was my mother's room," Dixie said. "She picked out the paper. The other bedroom has fire trucks and police cars on the walls."

Isi strolled over to the window. She spotted Conway in the midst of his brothers and their girlfriends, but it was Will who her boys stood next to. Will played quarterback and Javier and Miguel blocked for him. When the ball was snapped, Buck and Merle—called Mack by family and friends—tackled the twins to the ground. Her heart ached at the thought that she and her sons would never be part of this family. "The boys haven't had this much fun in a long while."

Dixie peeked over Isi's shoulder. "They're sweet kids."

"They don't get a chance to roughhouse very often." Isi's attention shifted to Conway. Maybe she was biased, but he was by far the handsomest of the males playing football. Each Cash brother was charming in their own way, but Conway was special—he was…or had been for a short time…her Cash brother.

"You'd think my siblings would have changed the wallpaper or painted over it, but since my mother had picked it out…" Dixie shrugged.

"Conway told me that your mother passed away when you were all young."

"It was a difficult time, but Johnny was our rock, and we had our grandparents."

Sensing Dixie would rather not discuss her mother, Isi asked, "Where did you sleep, if your brothers used these two rooms?"

"Follow me." Dixie walked to a door at the end of the hall. "This used to be an old linen closet. When I came along, Grandpa Ely knocked out the back wall of the closet and sealed off a portion of the attic, turning it into a bedroom for me." Dixie ducked inside and Isi followed.

"This is adorable." Isi's gaze took in the slanted ceiling and stained-glass window near the roof line. A second window had been cut into the side of the house to hold an air conditioner. "You must have felt like a princess in a castle tower."

"You're the only one who's ever come in here and said that. My brothers view it as a cramped, unappealing attic," Dixie said.

"This is definitely a girl's room and it should never be changed."

"I agree. Let me show you the bathroom. It has all the original fixtures."

When they stepped into the hallway, the bathroom door opened and Shannon emerged, her skin pale.

Dixie rushed forward, but Shannon held up a hand. "Don't say a word."

"How far along are you?" Dixie asked.

"Two months, but—" Shannon wiped at a tear that escaped her eye.

"But," Isi said, her expression softening. "Because Dixie had a miscarriage you're afraid it might happen to you, too."

Dixie frowned. "Conway told you?"

Isi nodded.

"It's true, Dix. I've been so worried, thinking about what you went through. I don't want to tell Johnny until I'm sure everything will be okay. All he talks about is how cute Nate is and how it would be fun having our own baby." Shannon winced. "He's got my father pestering me for grandchildren."

"I thought you were going to wait to start a family?"

"We were, but…"

"Johnny really wants to be a father," Dixie said. "He misses riding herd over me and our brothers."

Isi wished Conway felt the same about fatherhood.

"Then by all means have kids now if it'll keep Johnny from sticking his nose in our business," Dixie said.

"I want to surprise him at Christmas with the news."

"Don't worry." Dixie hugged Shannon. "Isi and I will keep your secret. In the meantime, smile and enjoy the moment. You're pregnant!"

The women went outside and Dixie took over watching Nate so Gavin could play football. Shannon sat on the swing with Dixie while Isi retrieved her disposable camera from her purse and snapped pictures of the game. This was the first Thanksgiving she and the boys hadn't spent alone, and she wanted more Conway memories for their scrapbooks.

Will stepped back to pass, but when he released the ball, Porter got his fingers on it, changing the flight path and sending it straight at Isi. Instinctively she put her hands out to protect her face and ended up catching the ball.

"Run, Isi, run!" Will shouted.

She raced down the steps and darted past hands that tried to capture her. Miguel and Javier ran alongside her then Will came out of nowhere. He scooped her into his arms and dodged his brothers. Isi clung to his neck, the football smashed between their bodies. When they whizzed past Conway, she caught him gaping.

Mack dove at them and Will stumbled. Isi buried her face in his neck and squeezed her eyes closed, bracing for impact. Right before they hit the ground, Will spun and Isi landed on top of him. Hanging on to her, he rolled Isi over the goal line and everyone erupted into cheers. Will broke out in laughter and she joined in. After a minute, he crawled to his feet and helped her off the ground then twirled her in the air.

"You won the game for us, Isi!" Will flashed a cocky grin at Conway who strode toward them.

"What the heck are you doing?" Conway said.

Isi attempted to step aside, but Will's arm tightened like a steel band against her waist.

"What do you mean, what am I doing?" Will said. "I'm celebrating our victory." He smiled at Isi as he slid his hand over her hip. "We make a great team, don't we?"

"That's cheating." Conway grabbed Isi by the arm and tugged her free of Will's hold.

Isi gasped. The two brothers weren't aware that everyone had stopped playing to watch them.

Will pulled Isi back to his side. "I didn't cheat."

"Yes, you did." Conway claimed her again.

"Isi's catch was made fair and square." This time when Will reached for her, Johnny stepped between the brothers.

"I get the feeling that you two aren't talking football anymore." Johnny narrowed his eyes. "It's Thanksgiving. Behave."

Miguel and Javier wiggled their way between the adults and hugged Isi. "You won the game, Mom!" Miguel gave her a high five.

"Next year Isi's on our team." Will's gaze challenged Conway.

"Time for dessert!" Dixie hollered from the porch.

"Before everyone fills up on pumpkin pie, we nee

to take a vote on whether or not any of us are interested in selling out to Bell Farms."

"You know where I stand," Conway said then walked toward the barn.

Isi rushed after him. Before she left she wanted to tell him that she'd found a new sitter. "Conway!"

He stopped and waited for her to catch up. "I need to talk to you." When he didn't say anything, she asked, "Show me the pond?"

"Can we come, too?" Miguel skidded to a stop at Isi's side.

"Can we, Conway?" Javier asked.

"Lead the way." He motioned for the boys to walk ahead. He wasn't in the best mood—not after watching Will plaster himself all over Isi as if she belonged to him.

Jealous?

Damn straight he was jealous. Some brother Will turned out to be—honing in on Isi. Conway should have never asked his brother to take her out on a date.

Then why did you?

Because I thought he was harmless! Will was supposed to have been a safe bet—a guy Conway could trust to show Isi a good time, not steal her out from under him.

You have no claim on her.

He'd made love to Isi—that meant she was off-limits to his brothers—no exceptions.

As they strolled along the path that skirted the barn, Conway couldn't ignore how much he'd missed Isi the past few days. Why did she have to be the one who touched him in a way no other woman ever had? If he could go back in time and intercept the punch Bridget had thrown at Isi's nose, he would. Then all would be right in his world.

"I wanted you to know that I found a sitter for the boys," she said.

"Who?"

"My neighbor Mrs. Sneed agreed to watch them."

"Will she drive the boys to school and pick them up?"

"Yes."

"And she's willing to stay late when you work at the bar?"

"Yes, but the boys will have to sleep at her house until I get home."

"Why can't they sleep in their own beds?"

"Mrs. Sneed won't give up her television programs, and I don't have satellite TV." Isi continued walking. "The boys will fall asleep quickly once they're back in their own beds."

Conway didn't like the new arrangement for the twins.

You're not their father. You don't have a say. Before he pestered Isi with more questions about her neighbor, the boys raced toward the pond.

"Wait for us!" he shouted. Once they reached the water's edge, he said, "Stay here." Conway walked the perimeter of the pond then announced, "Coast is clear."

"What were you doing?" she asked.

"Searching for snakes."

Isi held fast to the boys' shirt collars. "Are you sure it's safe?"

"Positive. I haven't seen a snake in months. Not since Porter and Buck cleared out a den a mile from here last spring."

She released her hold on the twins. "You can stick your toes in the water, but don't get your clothes wet."

Mig and Javi removed their shoes and socks then waded a few feet into the water, squealing at the cold temperature.

"I can't thank you enough for all the help you've given me this semester," she said. "I don't know what I would have done if you hadn't stepped up after Nicole left me high and dry."

"I was glad to help."

"Now you can get back to farming and not worry about interruptions."

He'd finished the pecan harvest. All that remained to do was clean up the debris in the grove and next month prune the dead branches from the trees. He wouldn't be doing any of that if his siblings voted to sell out tonight.

As if Isi read his mind, she asked, "What was Johnny talking about when he said you were all supposed to cast a vote on selling the farm?"

"An agricultural company made an offer to buy the orchards."

"You don't think they'll sell, do you?"

"I don't know. I'm the only one who's willing to harvest the pecans."

"I can't picture your sister getting rid of the farmhouse. She loves your grandmother's home."

"I'll find out later tonight."

"If they decide to sell, what will you do?"

"Go back on the rodeo circuit full-time." The prospect didn't excite him.

He changed the subject. "When's your graduation ceremony?"

"They don't have one for students who finish school in December."

That wasn't right. Isi had worked her butt off to earn a degree. She deserved to celebrate her success. His gaze cut to the boys. Who would throw Isi a party—she had no family and her best friend was in California.

"Hey, Conway," Miguel said. "Can we ride on your tractor?"

Now that Isi no longer needed him to babysit this might be the last time Miguel and Javier visited the farm. No more tractor rides. No more naps in the hammock. No more visits to the pond. "Sure. We better head back before it gets dark."

The boys giggled and fell backward as they struggled to pull their socks on over wet feet.

Isi watched with a wry smile. "They're a riot, aren't they?"

Conway chuckled, but his chest felt as if it was cracking wide open. He was going to miss the little troublemakers more than he'd ever imagined.

Chapter Twelve

"I don't like Mrs. Sneed. She has bad breath," Miguel said.

Her son made their neighbor sound like a troll who lived under a bridge. "It's not nice to talk about people like that."

The Monday after Thanksgiving was proving to be a difficult one. The boys had been down in the dumps all weekend since they'd learned their neighbor would be babysitting them.

"How long does Mrs. Sneed gotta watch us?" Javier shoved a bite of hot dog into his mouth.

"I'll be finished with school in three weeks. Hopefully it won't be long before I find a new job and I'm able to stay home at night with you guys."

Miguel grunted as he carried his empty plate to the sink.

"Is Red gonna be mad if you get a new job?" Javier asked.

"No, honey. He wants me to use the skills I learned in school."

Javier took his plate to the sink. "What skills?"

"Stuff I learned how to do on the computer. Like keep track of product sales, orders and inventory."

"What's a product?" Javier asked.

"An item that a business sells. A product at Red's bar would be a cheeseburger basket."

Javier came back to the table and sat down. "Are toys products?"

"Yes."

"Are we gonna get products for Christmas?" Miguel asked.

"I'm sure Santa will bring you a toy."

Javier shook his head. "Katie said Santa isn't real."

The boys' classmate was supposedly the smartest kid at their school. By the time she'd turned two, she'd probably figured out Santa Claus was a myth.

"You'll have to wait until Christmas morning to see that Santa isn't a fake."

"Can we get a real tree this year?" Miguel asked.

She almost caved in just to erase the hangdog expressions from their faces. "No real tree but we'll string up Christmas lights on the trailer like we did last year." There was no money in the budget for a real tree or an artificial one—not if she hoped to purchase Christmas gifts.

"Get your backpacks and I'll walk you over to Mrs. Sneed's."

Isi prayed this day would go well and that the older woman would have patience with the twins, because if things didn't work out, she'd end up having to bring the boys to school with her and that was a no-win situation for everyone.

"How come you let the twins color with their crayons all over the porch floor?" Will asked when he stopped next to Conway in front of the farmhouse.

"I didn't let them. They got bored with their coloring

books." He shrugged. "It wasn't a big deal. The porch needed painting anyway."

Will motioned to the paint can in Conway's hand. "You're going to need more than one coat to cover the marks."

"I think I can handle this." He scowled. "What are you doing at the farm in the middle of the day?"

"I stopped by to pick up a shovel then I'm heading back out." Will glanced behind him. "Where are the twins?"

"In school." Conway hadn't told anyone that he'd stopped watching the boys. He wasn't sure if it was because he didn't want to answer their nosey questions or because he thought he might change his mind and reapply for the job.

"I get a kick out of the boys. Miguel never stops talking and—"

"What are your intentions toward Isi?" Conway set the paint can on the ground and faced his brother.

"What are you talking about?"

"You're always over at her trailer making repairs," Conway said.

"I've been helping her out. So what? I enjoy her company. She's easy to talk to."

Conway had been miffed at his brother since Thanksgiving when the twins had ignored him and followed Will around the farm all day like lost puppies. He'd didn't like being replaced.

Will eyed him suspiciously. "As a matter of fact, I'd planned to ask Isi out on a third date."

A burning sensation spread through Conway's chest. "Isi's not the kind of girl you date casually, Will. She's got kids. She needs a guy who'll be a good father to the twins not a guy who only wants to get into her bed."

"Who said I want to get into her bed?" Will grinned. "Not that I'd ever turn down an invitation from a pretty girl like—"

Before he realized what he was doing, Conway swung his fist, the punch hitting Will in the jaw. His brother stumbled backward and landed on his rump.

"What the hell did you do that for?" Will rubbed his jaw.

"Don't use Isi for sex." Conway was more worried that Isi might want to use Will to warm her bed than the other way around.

Will stared thoughtfully at Conway. "You're in love with her, aren't you?" he said.

No! Yes! "Maybe." He'd marry Isi in a heartbeat, but she had the twins…and Conway wasn't good enough to be their father. The boys deserved a man who would never turn his back on them.

Will got to his feet and brushed the seat of his pants off. "What's keeping you from asking her to marry you?"

"It wouldn't work out in the end." No way was he bringing up his long-ago visit with his birth father. It wasn't that he didn't think Will would understand or be sympathetic—after all, Will had grown up without a father, too. It had more to do with Conway's insecurities.

"If you're not willing to take a chance on Isi, then you're going to have to let her and the boys go, Conway. I'll tell you right now, there's probably more than one guy out there who'd give anything to make a life for himself with a woman like her. It's only a matter of time before that guy finds her." Will brushed past Conway and headed to the barn. "And by the way, next time you sucker punch me, I'm going to kick your ass."

A minute later, he emerged with a shovel and dropped the tool into his truck bed.

Will opened the driver's-side door. "Any luck selling the pecans?"

Conway's siblings had voted to keep the farm in the family and had given him complete control over managing the orchards. Now it was up to him to find a buyer for this year's crop. "I've got two bids. I'm waiting on a third then I'll decide."

"Good luck."

Conway had a feeling his brother's well-wishes were meant for him and Isi and not the pecans. Before his brother's truck had cleared the yard, Conway's cell phone rang. He didn't recognize the number.

"Conway Cash."

"Mr. Cash this is Sandy London. I work at the Tiny Tot Learn and Play preschool."

Why was the school calling him?

"Javier and Miguel picked a fight on the playground, and they're being sent home for the day. We called their mother, but she isn't answering her phone."

"Isi's in class right now," he said.

"You're listed as an emergency contact. Would you be able to come get the boys?"

"I thought Isi's neighbor Mrs. Sneed was dropping them off and picking them up now?"

"She's not answering her phone, either."

"I'll be there as soon as I can," Conway said.

"Thank you, Mr. Cash."

He disconnected the call then jogged to his truck. Wait until Isi found out the boys had been in another fight. She was going to be spitting mad—at him. He'd been the one to tell the twins to stand up for themselves and not allow bullies to threaten them.

The drive into Yuma took longer than usual—probably because his mind wouldn't stop envisioning Isi and Will together. By the time he turned into the school parking lot he was in a bad mood. He sat in the truck and took several deep breaths, willing himself to calm down before he went into the school to get the boys.

When he entered the building, Mig and Javi were sitting in the waiting room slouched in their chairs gazing at the ceiling lights. He cleared his throat and the woman behind the desk set aside the magazine she'd been reading. He waited for the boys to smile at him, but they ignored him.

He was no longer a hero in their eyes.

"I'm Conway Cash," he said.

"Hello, Mr. Cash. Please sign here that you're taking Miguel and Javier home." She handed him a clipboard. "Thank you for coming to get them."

He scribbled his name on the paper then spoke to the boys. "Your mother isn't going to be happy about this."

Heads held high, the twins marched outside. As soon as the door shut behind them, Javier said, "What are we gonna do?"

"We're going back to the trailer to tell Mrs. Sneed she doesn't need to pick you up this afternoon."

"This sucks," Miguel said.

Conway was sure Isi didn't allow the boys to say the word *suck,* but he didn't reprimand Miguel, because… well, because.

They made the drive to the mobile-home park in silence. Conway struggled not to laugh at the boys' sullen expressions. He wanted to say he was proud they'd stood up for themselves, but he doubted Isi would approve.

Conway parked next to the trailer and helped the boys out of the backseat then motioned for them to sit on the porch steps. "Wait there." He cut across the yard to the neighbor's trailer.

Mrs. Sneed answered the door on the second knock. "Who are you?"

"My name is Conway Cash, ma'am. I'm a friend of Isi's."

The old woman nodded. "You're the young man who watched the boys for Isi."

"Yes, ma'am." Conway explained what had happened at the school.

"I don't answer my phone when my game shows are on," she said.

Did Isi know that? "I was listed as one of the emergency contacts."

"Are you taking care of the boys then?" she asked. "My game shows won't be over for a while."

"I'll watch them until Isi gets home tonight."

The relief on Mrs. Sneed's face suggested that she regretted offering to watch the boys. "Thank you," she said then closed the door.

When Conway returned to Isi's yard, the twins looked bored. He sat on the bottom step and stretched out his legs. "Okay, let's hear it."

"Hear what?" Miguel asked.

"The reason you started a fight at recess."

Javier surprised Conway by speaking up first. "Katie said that Santa Claus is a fake."

"You fought with a girl?" Conway asked.

"No." Javier nudged Miguel and his brother explained.

"Katie told everyone that Santa was a fake and Rico got mad and shoved her and she fell and skinned her knee."

"And she cried," Javier said.

Conway was losing track of the conversation. "So who did you get into a fight with?"

"Rico," Miguel said. "Javi pushed Rico 'cause he pushed Katie and you told me I had to stick up for Javi so I pushed Rico, too."

"And let me guess," Conway said. "The recess monitor only saw you and Javi push Rico."

Both boys nodded.

"So did Rico get in trouble for pushing Katie?" Conway asked.

"Katie told our teacher that Rico started it, but we still got in trouble," Javier said.

"I'm glad you stuck up for Katie. Boys should never ever hurt girls," Conway said.

"We know. Our mom told us that." Javier bumped his brother's shoulder again.

"Is Santa really a fake?" Miguel asked.

Oh, boy. "What do you think?" Conway asked.

"Mom said Santa was real." Miguel looked at his brother.

"But if Santa's real then how come we only get one toy from our wish list and other kids get lots more?" Javier blinked his innocent brown eyes at Conway.

"Is it 'cause our mom doesn't have a lot of money?" Miguel asked.

"Money has nothing to do with Santa Claus."

"Katie said that Santa's elves aren't real and they don't make toys. She said moms and dads go to the store and buy the toys." Miguel sucked in a breath. "Is it 'cause we don't got a dad to buy us presents?"

The kid sure knew how to twist the knife in Conway's chest. He opened his mouth to contradict Katie's claim, but Javier interrupted him.

"Can you give our mom money? Then she can buy us lots of toys at the store."

"Or you can buy us a Christmas tree," Miguel said.

They weren't getting a tree—Christmas wasn't Christmas without a tree. Before he had a chance to answer the boys, Isi's car turned into the trailer park. Saved by the bell. "Time to face the music, guys."

"ANOTHER FIGHT?" ISI GLANCED between her sons.

The twins studied their shoes and avoided eye contact with their mother. Conway sympathized with the boys but refrained from intervening. He'd meddled enough in their lives.

Isi shifted her attention to Conway. "I wasn't able to check my phone messages until after class, or I would have been here sooner. I'm sorry you had to drive all the way into Yuma to pick them up from school."

"I was happy to help out." That was the truth. Conway couldn't deny that he'd missed the boys and Isi. A whole lot more than he'd expected to.

"Go to your room right now. We'll discuss your behavior in a minute." Hands on her hips she glared until the twins trudged inside the trailer. Once the door closed behind them, she said, "I owe you an apology. I forgot to ask the school to remove your name as an emergency contact."

Conway stared at Isi, thinking something seemed different about her. "Seriously, Isi, it was no trouble—"

"Yes, it was trouble," she said.

"That's what's different about you." He snapped his fingers. "You're wearing your hair down." Isi usually put her long hair in a ponytail. His mind flashed back to the night he'd spent in her bed, running his hands through the silky strands. "You should leave your hair loose more often. It's beautiful."

Blushing, she changed the subject. "Why couldn't Mrs. Sneed get the boys?"

"She said she doesn't answer the phone when her game shows are on."

"Great." Isi's shoulders sagged, as if she carried the weight of the world on them. The urge to hug her was strong, but he doubted his sympathy would be welcome.

"Did the boys tell you what the fight was about?" she asked.

"Santa Claus."

"What?"

He patted the step and she sat next to him. The faint scent of her perfume triggered an image of her naked body in his mind. He shifted on the step, hoping to hide his growing arousal. Making love to Isi had released two years of pent-up desire for her and reining it back in was damn near impossible.

"What about Santa Claus?" she asked.

"A kid at school said there wasn't a Santa Claus and that moms and dads bought the toys."

Isi blinked hard.

He grasped her hand—not to offer comfort but because he had to touch her—he'd missed that intimate connection with her.

"They figured it out, didn't they?" she whispered.

"Figured what out?"

"That they get one gift at Christmas, because I don't make enough money to buy more."

"The boys have plenty of toys." He gestured to the box by the shed.

"But they're second-hand toys. Cast-offs from other kids."

He snuggled her against his side. This felt so right—him and Isi. Why couldn't he find the courage to take a leap of faith and commit to her? "You're doing the best you can for the boys. When they grow up and understand the sacrifices you've made, they'll love you even more."

"Or they'll resent me for making bad choices."

"What bad choices?"

"I made the decision to come to America with nothing but a suitcase full of clothes. Then I slept with a married man and got pregnant."

"Cut yourself some slack, Isi. You were vulnerable and scared."

"Stop being nice. I was stupid to believe Tyler really cared for me."

Conway wasn't used to doling out advice—he was used to seeking Isi's counsel. "I think you'll be happy when you hear the reason the boys got into a fight today."

"You don't have to protect them," she said.

"I'm not. Javier shoved Rico because Rico pushed Katie to the ground after she told everyone at recess that there was no Santa Claus."

Isi smiled. "Javier stood up for Katie?"

"Yep. And when Rico shoved Javi back, Miguel stepped in and shoved Rico hard enough that the kid fell down and the recess monitor saw them."

"I'm proud of Javi for trying to protect Katie," Isi said.

"And I'm the one who told Miguel that he should always have his brother's back on the playground."

She shook her head. "So you encouraged the boys to fight rather than talk out their disagreements with other kids?"

"Kids this age don't talk, Isi. Besides, fighting was the only way I knew how to defend myself when I was in school."

"What do you mean?"

"My grandpa never taught me how to handle the ribbing I got because of my name. Johnny was the one who looked out for us."

"Johnny taught you to fight?"

"He didn't exactly teach me. I picked it up from watching him defend my brothers against bullies."

"You never told me you were teased."

"With a name like Conway Twitty Cash I've had my share of fights. Though I count myself lucky I wasn't the one named Merle. It's no wonder my brother goes by Mack."

"Why in the world did your mother name you all after country and western singers?"

"Grandma claimed that when our mom was a teenager, she'd lock herself in her bedroom and listen to the music of all the country-western greats."

"She must have known saddling you with those old-fashioned names would cause trouble."

"Our mom was never there when one of us came home from school with a black eye." And when his mother had been at the farm, she hadn't asked her children about their friends or problems they were having in school.

"Defending my name with my fists became second nature. My brothers and I were all suspended from school for fighting at least once. Johnny spent the most time in the principal's office, because he fought our battles for us until we became old enough to hold our own."

"Do people still mock your name?"

"Once in a while, but now I disarm the big-boy

bullies with my smile and charm." He sobered. "I'm sorry if I overstepped my bounds, but the twins need to learn to stand up for themselves. If they don't, the bullying might snowball until one of them really gets hurt."

"I'll talk to the supervisor at the school and figure out where we go from here." She motioned to his truck. "I don't want to keep you any longer."

"I'm not in any hurry to leave." There was nothing waiting for him at the farm except an orchard full of nut trees.

She smiled. "I landed a job interview."

"When?"

"Next Thursday after my final exam. A stationery store in Yuma needs an office manager."

"Manager? That sounds impressive."

"Not really. I'd be sitting in a back room on the computer all day, but the position comes with benefits."

"Will Mrs. Sneed watch the boys while you go to the interview?"

"She's supposed to. The interview is at four-thirty then afterward, I have to work at the bar until midnight."

"I hope the interview goes well."

"Thanks. This could be a new beginning for me and the boys."

Conway forced a smile, but the future appeared anything but promising—at least for him. Isi would nail the job interview. She'd quit waitressing for Red. He'd no longer drop by the bar, because she wouldn't be there to talk to. And their friendship would fade into a fond memory.

Exactly what you want, right?

"I better get going," he said.

Isi walked him to his truck. "Thank you for being there for the boys."

He *had* been there for the boys, hadn't he? "Keep me as an emergency contact."

"You sure?"

"Positive." He toyed with his keys. "Maybe I could take the boys next Thursday, while you're at school and the interview. We could do guy stuff at the farm." Conway expected Isi to jump at the offer—her hesitation felt like a punch in the gut.

"I don't know if that's a good idea, Conway. They took it pretty hard when I told them you wouldn't be babysitting anymore."

He understood Isi's concern. He'd hurt the boys when he'd backed away, but he wasn't ready to say goodbye— not yet. "I'd like to make it up to them."

"I suppose the boys can skip school that day. Their class Christmas party is on Monday then most of the kids will be no-shows the rest of the week, because their parents are on vacation."

"What time should I pick them up?"

"Nine-thirty would be great then I can get to school early and study before my test."

"See you at nine-thirty." Conway hopped into his truck and drove off. When he adjusted his side mirror and saw Isi standing by the carport, a sharp pain struck his chest.

Leaving her didn't feel right.

"What's Conway gonna do with us, Mom?" Javier asked as Isi tied his shoes.

"I'm not sure, honey." The second Thursday in December had arrived and she'd almost phoned Conway and canceled his plans with the boys. She was torn between wanting them to have this last memory with their favorite sitter and wanting to protect them from feeling abandoned when Conway didn't come by again after today.

And she admitted she was being selfish—she wanted to see Conway one more time, too.

"How come you're not going with us?" Miguel asked.

"My final exam is this afternoon."

"Are you gonna get an A?" Javier asked.

"I hope so." Isi had lectured the boys until she was blue in the face about the importance of getting a good education, and she had proudly shared her grades with them—As, Bs and the few Cs she'd earned.

"Conway's here!" Miguel shouted from his post at the front window. He raced outside, Javier following him.

Isi ducked into the bathroom to touch up her makeup and hair. She wore black dress pants and a silky blouse with a blazer for her interview after class. She'd secured her hair in a clip on top of her head, the style making her appear older and more confident than she felt. When she emerged from the bathroom, Conway stood in the living room answering a barrage of questions from the boys.

"Where are we going?" Javier asked.

Miguel tugged on Conway's pant leg. "Can we drive the tractor?"

"Stop harassing Conway." Isi smiled.

Conway did a double-take when he saw her. "Wow. You look nice."

"Thanks. I won't have time to change clothes before the interview, so I'm stuck wearing this to school."

"Good luck with the test and the interview," he said.

She gathered her backpack and purse. "Be good for Conway and use your manners." She hugged the boys.

Conway grinned. "Don't I get one?"

"I suppose." Playing along, she stood on tiptoe and hugged Conway only he turned his head toward her and their lips bumped. She stepped back quickly but the boys caught the kiss.

"Hey, I want a kiss," Javier said.

"Me, too." Miguel stuck out his face.

Isi made a big production out of kissing the boys' cheeks then beat a hasty retreat, closing the door behind her.

"We have a lot to do," Conway said.

"You got lipstick on your face." Miguel smiled.

He rubbed his fingers over the sticky gloss on his mouth. "Is it gone?"

Javier nodded then said, "Is mine gone?" He rubbed his cheek.

"Yep. Now, here's the plan. We're throwing a graduation party for your mom."

The boys' eyes rounded. "What's a graduation party?" Miguel asked.

"It's a party to celebrate when a person finishes high school or college."

Javier clapped his hands. "I like parties."

"I talked to Red, and he said we can have the party at the bar. When your mom goes to work after her job interview, we'll all be there to surprise her. First, we need to shop for decorations."

"Do we gotta get a cake, too?" Miguel asked.

"Good thinking. We'll stop at the grocery store and pick one out."

"She likes flowers on cakes," Javier said then in the same breath asked, "Does she get presents?"

Conway hadn't thought about gifts. "Do you want to buy your mom a gift?"

Both boys shouted, "Yes!"

"What should we buy her?" Conway asked.

"A new vacuum," Javier said.

"She yells at ours 'cause it doesn't work," Miguel said.

A vacuum wasn't an exciting graduation gift. "We'll see." Maybe he'd think of the perfect present while they were shopping. "Get your jackets. We've got lots of errands to run before the big party."

Chapter Thirteen

Isi sat across from Mr. Buford's desk in a windowless room at the back of Buford's Stationery and Office Supply and waited patiently for him to read her résumé.

"The school courses you've taken are impressive." He set the paper aside. "But you have no work experience in an office environment."

"No, sir, I don't."

"And your current employer is the Border Town Bar & Grill."

"I waitress there at night. Taking classes during the day didn't leave me with many options for evening jobs that paid well."

"I don't know if you intend to keep your waitressing position on the weekends, but all of my employees work at least one Saturday a month."

"I plan to quit my current job and I'd make child-care arrangements for any Saturday I'm scheduled to work."

Mr. Buford's gaze shifted to her left hand. "Are you married, Ms. Lopez?"

Isi swallowed a sigh. Why had she brought up the boys? "No, sir."

"I was raised by a single mother."

His confession released the tension from Isi's body.

"Making ends meet was a daily struggle for her," he said.

"The difficult times are worth it. I wouldn't trade my life for the world. Everything I do is for my sons."

"Sons?"

She smiled. "Twin four-year-olds."

"What do you do with the boys when you're in school or working at the bar?"

This wasn't a typical interview. She worried Mr. Buford was judging her character and not her job skills. "The boys are in preschool during the afternoon and a neighbor watches them until I get home from the bar."

"No family?"

She shook her head.

"My mother was all alone, too." His attention shifted to the wall across the room. "I was a latch-key kid."

Isi wasn't sure what to say.

"I'm willing to hire you on a trial basis—three months. After that time, I'll evaluate your job performance and if all goes well, I'll make you a permanent employee and you'll be eligible for benefits."

Relief made Isi light-headed. "That sounds more than fair. What hours will I be working?"

"I'm going to leave that up to you. The store hours are Monday through Saturday eight to six. As long as you handle your responsibilities, you're free to work with your sons' schedules."

Isi reminded herself to be firm and confident when she stated her salary requirements. "I'd need at least twelve dollars an hour."

"I'll start you at fourteen dollars and if you stay on after three months, I'll pay you sixteen."

Never in her wildest dreams had she believed she'd make sixteen dollars an hour.

"I give all my employees a Christmas bonus and the amount depends on the total store sales for the year." He smiled. "Incentive for everyone to work hard."

For the first time in years an exciting future awaited her. All her sacrifices might finally pay off.

"You'll begin January second." Mr. Buford scribbled on a piece of paper and handed it to Isi. "My office phone number if you need to get in touch with me or leave a message."

"Thank you for this opportunity, Mr. Buford." She shook his hand. "You won't be sorry you hired me."

"It's a pleasure to have you as part of our team, Ms. Lopez."

As soon as Isi left the stationery store, she whooped for joy, but her excitement fizzled as she drove to work. Her life was taking a turn for the better, but this new path didn't include Conway. When she arrived at the bar, she noticed only a few cars parked in the lot, which was unusual for this time of day.

She grabbed her purse and Border Town Bar & Grill T-shirt then walked to the entrance, where she found the front door locked. Had Red scheduled an employee meeting that she'd forgotten about? She went behind the building and entered through the back door. The kitchen was dark.

"Anybody in here?" She pushed through the swinging door to the barroom.

"Surprise!"

Isi jumped inside her skin.

The lights popped on, and she gaped in shock at her coworkers who blew paper horns and threw streamers and confetti into the air. Then she spotted Conway and her sons standing in front of a banner that read Congratulations Graduate! Her eyes flooded with tears.

"Yeah, Mom!" Miguel yelled. Javier mimicked his brother and the rest of the room echoed "congratulations," "good job" and "way to go, Isi."

"I don't know what to say." She wiped at her tears.

"A toast to the new graduate." Conway raised his beer bottle and several cheers followed.

She smiled through her tears. "No one's ever thrown me a party."

More horns blew. Sasha fed quarters into the jukebox and Red waved her over to see her cake.

"The boys picked it out." Conway chuckled. "They asked the lady in the bakery to put lots of flowers on it."

Isi hugged her sons then Conway. "Thank you. This is turning out to be a great day." She smiled. "I got the job."

"That's awesome, Isi." Conway whistled and a hush fell over the bar. "Hey, everyone, listen up. Isi nailed the job interview and they hired her!"

More cheers and congratulations.

"We got you a present, Mom." Javier handed her a small jeweler's box.

Isi glanced at Conway, wondering if…

Don't be stupid. It's not an engagement ring.

She held her breath as she lifted the lid on the velvet case. A silver necklace with a star pendant. The air in her lungs leaked out and she widened her smile to hide her disappointment.

"It's beautiful, boys."

"Conway said if you wear it, you can reach the stars," Javier said.

"And the necklace will remind your mom that dreams only come true if you never stop dreaming."

Isi swallowed the lump in her throat. She couldn't very well tell Conway that the star wouldn't work, because her dream-come-true stood right in front of her yet remained out of reach.

"The necklace is lovely." The star would always remind her of what she yearned for but could never have. "Let's dance." She twirled the boys and others in the crowd joined them.

Time passed in a blur. Before Isi knew it seven o'clock had rolled around and Red opened the bar to the public after he'd told her to take the night off. She thanked her coworkers for coming to her graduation party and Conway carried the leftover cake to the car for her then retrieved the boys' booster seats from his truck.

"I think we surprised your mom tonight, didn't we, guys?"

"Were you surprised, Mom?" Javier asked.

"I was. This has been the best night ever."

Conway leaned his head inside the car after the boys crawled into their seats. "Be good for your mom."

"Are you gonna come to our house tomorrow?" Miguel asked.

"No, buddy. Now that your mom is finished with school, I won't be hanging out with you guys any longer. Don't worry, though, we'll see each from time to time."

It occurred to Isi that this was her and Conway's final goodbye.

Conway stepped away from the car but didn't make eye contact with her. "Put your belts on, guys." Isi shut the door, cutting off their protests.

"Thank you, Conway. I couldn't have made it through these past couple of months without your help." *Without you.*

"I enjoyed hanging out with the boys."

"Good luck finding 'the one.'" She forced a smile "I'll miss hearing about your trials and tribulations."

"I'll stop by the stationery store and keep you updated."

"Don't you dare." She laughed. "I don't want to lose my job." Keeping her smile in place she said, "When you do find 'the one,' it would be nice to know who she is."

"You'll be the first person I tell."

Isi couldn't stand it any longer. She hugged Conway hard then walked to the driver's side of the car.

"Isi?"

"What?"

"Take care of yourself and the boys."

"I will." She slid behind the wheel and drove off grateful their goodbye had been short. Tonight after she put the boys to bed and it sunk in that she'd not only lost the man she'd fallen in love with but also a good friend, she'd cry her eyes out.

"How come we gotta stay with Mrs. Sneed if you don't have to go to school?" Javier stood in the bathroom doorway Monday morning, watching Isi put on her makeup.

"Because you're on Christmas break and your school is closed this week." Red had switched Isi to the day shift at the bar and she planned to use her lunch hour to shop for Christmas toys.

"I don't want to go to Mrs. Sneed's, either." Miguel joined his brother in the doorway.

"She said she'd bake cookies with you."

"I don't like cookies." Miguel's petulant expression tested Isi's patience.

"Cheer up. Christmas Eve is three days away. Aren't you excited?"

"No." Miguel stomped off.

"What's wrong with Mig, Javi?"

"He's sad."

"Why?"

"'Cause Conway's gone."

The boys had already forgotten and forgiven Conway after he'd turned down their invitation to be their dad. She wished she could rebound so quickly from life's disappointments. "You two had a lot of fun with Conway, but he's got his own life to live and..." *He doesn't want us to be a part of it.* "We have our lives to live."

"Mom."

"What, Javi?"

"Can I change my Christmas wish list?"

She stopped applying her lipstick. "We already mailed your letter to Santa."

"I don't want a black Furby."

Good thing she hadn't bought the toy yet. "What do you want?"

"I want Conway to come back."

She finished putting on her lipstick then knelt in front of her son. "Conway can't watch you anymore."

Javier leaned against her and she hugged him. If there truly was a Santa Claus, then she'd have put Conway on her wish list, too. Javier touched the star pendant she wore. "Can we wish for Santa to bring Conway back?"

"I'm afraid Santa only delivers toys to children, not wishes."

"Conway said if we wished hard enough our wishes will come true," he said.

Isi wasn't a big fan of wish-making. After her father had disappeared, her mother had told her that if she wished hard enough for his return, one day he would come home. All those years of wishing had been for nothing. "Go play with Miguel. I'll walk you over to Mrs. Sneed's in a minute."

After Javier left the bathroom, she closed her eyes and willed the tears not to fall. How long would it be, before her and the boys' hearts finally let go of Conway?

"WHO DIED?"

Conway shifted his gaze to the barn doorway where his brother Johnny stood.

"No one died. Why?"

"You don't normally grimace like that." Johnny walked farther into the barn and stopped next to the tractor. "What are you doing?"

"Testing the fluids."

"Did Dixie tell you that we're all gathering at the Triple D for Christmas this year?"

"Nope." His sister had left him a voicemail message last night, but he hadn't listened to it, because he hadn't been in the mood to talk to anyone.

"Shannon's brothers will be there and Clive's bringing Fiona Wilson."

"Your father-in-law is still dating the town spinster?"

"He doesn't talk about her and I don't ask questions." Johnny picked up a wrench from the toolbox and examined it.

"Shouldn't you be out punching cows or training horses?" Conway asked.

"I needed a break."

"Trouble in paradise?"

"Shannon's been cranky lately."

"Why?"

"I don't have any idea. When I mention her mood, she bites my head off."

Before he met Isi, Conway had believed himself an expert on women. Now, he didn't have a clue.

"Speaking of women, why aren't you watching Isi's boys?"

"She graduated from the community college and starts a new job next month." For a man who'd been dead set against having kids, not an hour in the day passed by when Javier and Miguel didn't cross his mind. The boys had weaseled their way into his heart and the thought of never hanging out with them again left a hollow feeling in his chest.

"Good for Isi," Johnny said. "I hope things work out for her."

So did Conway.

Johnny turned to leave then stopped. "I almost forgot to tell you. Dixie and Gavin bought a house in Yuma. The closing is in January and she wants our help moving."

"I'll be here." Where else did he have to go? After Johnny left, Conway sat in the barn a while longer and reflected on his life. He'd taken over the farm, and with the added responsibility he'd discovered that he enjoyed being the caretaker of his grandfather's orchards. This year's harvest had been a lot of work, but the bond he'd developed with the land fulfilled him in a way nothing else had—not even rodeo. He thought he'd miss riding the circuit, but the time he'd spent on the farm with Javier and Miguel had been his best days.

Maybe he should resume his mission to find "the one." He waited for the rush of adrenaline that usually hit him when he made plans to prowl the honky tonks, but the blood pumping through his veins felt sluggish.

Calling it quits for the day he returned to the bunkhouse to shower and change. He decided to drive into town and shop. He didn't exchange holiday gifts with his siblings, but he wanted to buy a toy for his nephew's first Christmas.

An image of Javier and Miguel flashed through Conway's mind. The boys were the perfect age to enjoy Christmas. They still believed in Santa Claus and he envisioned them tearing the wrapping paper from their gifts with lightning speed.

Not an hour of the day passed by when Conway didn't regret how he'd handled the situation with Javier and Miguel when they'd asked him to be their father. He'd hurt them deeply and he wanted to make it up to the boys so they wouldn't remember him in a bad light. There was no reason why he couldn't buy them a couple of Christmas gifts, too.

An hour later, Conway had showered and left the farm. As he mulled over options for gifts, his truck sped past a parked van that had pulled off the road ten miles outside of Yuma. A sign next to the vehicle read Black Labs 4-Sale.

The boys would love a dog.

Giving no thought to how Isi might feel about owning a dog, Conway made a U-turn and drove back to the van.

"How much?" he asked, studying the five puppies inside a makeshift pen.

"A hundred dollars. They're American labs, not English," the woman said.

"What's the difference?" Conway didn't know a thing about the breed.

"American labs have a longer nose and thinner body but they're more energetic."

Energetic was good. The dog would be able to keep up with the boys. Conway watched the puppies interact—four of them attempted to climb out of the pen and one hung back, watching the others. The shy puppy made Conway think of Javier. He pulled his wallet from his pocket and shelled out the money. "I'll take the one in the corner."

"That's a male."

The woman set the puppy inside a cardboard box with an old towel at the bottom before taking Conway's cash. "Be sure he sees a vet soon for a physical and his vaccinations."

"Thanks." Back on the road, Conway pushed the speed limit into Yuma—he couldn't wait to see the expressions on the boys' faces when he handed them their Christmas present.

"How come you came to get us?" Miguel followed Conway across Mrs. Sneed's yard, Javier trailing him.

"I have an early Christmas present for you." Mrs. Sneed had gladly handed over the boys and their booster seats for the afternoon after Conway promised to return them to her before Isi got off work at six.

"What kind of surprise?" Javier grasped Conway's hand. His small fingers felt fragile and Conway's chest tightened with an unexpected need to protect the kid.

"This kind of surprise." He stopped at the truck and opened the door. The boys gasped when they saw the puppy's face peeking over the edge of the box.

"Is he ours?" Miguel asked.

"Yep." Conway carried the box to the middle of the yard and sat on the ground. When he set the puppy free, the lab tried to climb the boys' legs. The twins took turns holding the dog and giggling when it licked their faces.

"What's his name?" Javier asked.

"He doesn't have one. You two need to come up with a name for him."

"How come you gave us a dog?" Miguel squealed when the puppy pawed at his hair.

"Because all little boys should grow up with a dog." And because the dog would be there for the boys for the rest of its life—unlike Conway.

"Missy has a dog named Pringles," Miguel said.

"Who's Missy?"

"She lives with her grandma across the street," Javi said.

Miguel petted the dog. "We can call him Captain America."

"That's dumb." Javier shoved his brother's shoulder. Miguel shoved back. "You're dumb."

"No fighting. You can think of names while we run errands." Conway put the dog in the box.

"Where are we going?" Miguel asked.

"The puppy needs to see a doctor to make sure he's healthy." Conway knew of one pet store that had a veterinary clinic inside it. He'd gone there once with a girlfriend whose cat had become sick.

After the boys were belted in, Conway drove across town. The vet appointment took an hour and the puppy passed inspection. A vet tech talked Conway into purchasing pet insurance to cover neutering, yearly vaccinations and dental care.

Puppy supplies were next on the list. The boys selected a red collar and leash. Conway tossed an extra collar into the basket, warning the boys that the dog would outgrow the smaller one in a few months. The boys asked how big the dog would get and Conway found a book with pictures of full-grown labs.

"He's gonna be big," Javier said.

"Big enough to handle you two." Conway put the book into the cart, in case Isi had questions on training the dog. "Next, we need food and chew toys."

By the time he rolled the shopping cart up to the counter, the basket was overflowing. He'd purchased enough food to last three months, because he didn't want the dog to be a financial burden on Isi.

He and the boys hauled their stash to the truck then returned to the trailer where Conway laid Isi's ironing board across the floor in front of the bathroom and told the boys that the puppy would have to remain in the room until he was trained to do his business outside. Javier spread the piddle pads across the floor and Miguel filled the water bowl, then Conway set the puppy on his towel and he curled into a ball and went to sleep.

"Make sure you tell your mom that the vet said to feed the dog twice a day—once in the morning and once at suppertime. And you need to take him outside to do his job right after he eats, okay?"

"What's his job?" Javier asked.

"Poop. You don't want the dog to do that on the floor or on top of your bed."

"Eew!" Javier pinched his nose. "Yuck!"

"C'mon. Time to go to Mrs. Sneed's."

The boys didn't want to leave the puppy and spent ten more minutes saying goodbye before they followed Conway outside. After placing the house key in the potted plant on the porch, both Miguel and Javier hugged Conway's leg and thanked him for the puppy.

"Be good to your new best friend, okay?" Conway crouched in front of the boys. "Never hit the dog and never throw anything at him or tug on his legs or ears, okay?"

"We won't."

"You treat him kindly, and he'll be your friend for life." Conway stood.

"Are you gonna come back and see the puppy?" Javier asked.

"Probably not for a while." They walked in silence to the neighbor's trailer.

When Mrs. Sneed opened the door, Javier said, "Conway bought us a new puppy for Christmas."

After the boys went inside, Conway said, "The puppy's penned in the bathroom right now."

"Okay." Mrs. Sneed smiled and shut the door in his face, no doubt eager to get back to whatever TV program she was watching.

Conway considered waiting for Isi to return to warn her about the dog but he chickened out. After letting her and the boys down, there was no telling what he'd do or how far he'd go to make amends.

Chapter Fourteen

"Mom, you're gonna be excited about the present Conway got us for Christmas," Miguel said as he and his brother followed Isi to their trailer.

When she'd arrived at Mrs. Sneed's to pick up her sons, her neighbor informed her that Conway had spent the afternoon with the boys. Isi didn't know what to make of his visit or his buying her sons Christmas gifts.

As soon as she opened the door and stepped into the trailer, a tiny bark stopped her in her tracks.

Oh, no.

The boys raced down the hallway to the bathroom.

"It's a black lab," Javier said.

"I see." The puppy's tail wagged so hard his back end danced.

"Conway bought us a dog for Christmas and food and toys and bones." Javier went into the kitchen and returned with a folder of paperwork. "Our dog gets to go to the vet for free."

Conway had thought of everything, except who would take the dog outside during the middle of the day when she was at work and the boys were in school.

Miguel cuddled the puppy against his chest. The poignant picture tugged at her heart. The dog would go a long way in helping her sons cope with Conway's absence, but like her graduation necklace, the dog would always remind her of Conway. Emotions aside, this wasn't the right time in their lives to own a pet, not with her starting a new job.

"Maybe you should take him outside and see if he has to go to the bathroom."

"Conway said we have to feed him dinner first," Miguel said. "Then we take him outside so he doesn't poop in the house."

"Does he have a name?" she asked.

Javier spoke up. "We wanna name him Bandit."

"Why Bandit?"

"'Cause that's the name of Mr. Mighty's dog."

Mr. Mighty was a cartoon show the boys watched on Saturday mornings. Isi scratched the puppy behind his ears. "I guess you do look like a Bandit."

A half hour later the puppy had eaten and done his job and now slept between the boys on the floor while they played with their building blocks. Isi got out the camera and snapped a few photos for the infamous scrapbooks then paced the kitchen floor, debating how to handle the situation. They couldn't keep the dog. She didn't have the money to pay for food and treats and bones and then after a year she'd have to pay for vet bills. If she had to spend her savings on a dog, how was she supposed to buy a new car or move her and the boys into a nice apartment?

A lump formed in her throat as she watched the boys cuddle Bandit. She didn't want to be the bad guy and tell her sons that they couldn't keep the dog. Tomorrow, after she dropped them off at Mrs. Sneed's, she'd ask Conway to come get the dog.

CONWAY PULLED UP to Isi's trailer at three-thirty. She'd asked him to meet her at four. He got out of the truck and sat on the stoop to wait. He knew what this was about—the dog.

The strain in her voice when she'd left a message telling him she couldn't keep Bandit had been obvious. He'd overstepped his bounds. If he was honest, he'd admit that he'd only been thinking of himself when he'd gotten the dog for the boys. He'd felt bad that he'd walked out on the twins and had wanted to appease his guilt.

He worried about Javier and Miguel's reaction when they found out their mother wasn't going to let them keep Bandit. Everything he did only seemed to make things worse. He heard the clunking sound of Isi's car engine before she pulled beneath the carport. The boys hopped out of the backseat, wearing huge grins.

"Conway's here!" Javier scrambled up the porch steps and sat next to him.

"Did you come to see Bandit?" Miguel sat on the other side of Conway.

"We named him Bandit," Javier said.

Isi's brown eyes clouded with concern. She didn't say a word as she stepped past Javier and went into the trailer. He deserved her silence.

"He's getting bigger?" Miguel said.

Right then Isi opened the door and handed over the puppy then returned inside the trailer as if she couldn't stand to see her sons' faces when Conway broke the bad news.

The boys played with Bandit in the yard, their love for the dog obvious. Conway felt worse by the second. "Hey, guys. Bring Bandit over here and sit down."

Once they were settled on the steps and Bandit happily chewed on a bone, Conway said, "I have bad news."

The twins frowned.

"Bandit can't live at the trailer."

"Why not?" Miguel asked.

"It's my fault. I should have asked your mother if it was okay to give you guys a dog."

"But our mom likes Bandit," Javier said.

"Of course she does, but she works long hours and you two are in school during the day. Bandit's going to grow into a big dog and he needs more space to run around than this small yard."

Javier picked up the puppy and hugged him to his chest. "But he's ours. We don't want you to take him back."

Conway struggled to draw air into his lungs. "I'm not going to take him back."

"Where's he gonna go?" Miguel asked.

"He's going to live at the pecan farm. You guys can visit him anytime you want." For a man who was trying to break ties with this small family, he was failing miserably.

"But the farm is far away," Javier said.

"Bandit will have plenty of room to run at the farm. When you and your mom visit him, you can spend all day there, if you want."

"What if our mom won't take us to see Bandit?" Miguel asked.

"Then I'll bring him over to your house." Right now he'd do just about anything to erase the sad expressions on the boys' faces. "I promise I'll take good care of Bandit for you."

The trailer door opened and Isi stepped outside, her eyes darting between her sons. Javier hugged Bandit then set the puppy down and went inside. Miguel did the same, but as he passed his mother he glared and said, "You're mean."

"Isi, I'm sorry. I never meant for this to—"

She motioned to the storage shed. "Don't forget the bags of dog food and other supplies you bought."

So much for trying to make the boys' Christmas special—he'd ruined it instead.

"Is Nate having trouble sleeping again?" Conway asked Dixie as he climbed the porch steps.

"Yes." His sister patted the empty spot next to her on the swing.

"Kind of chilly out here to be rocking him, isn't it?"

"Nate's plenty warm in his blanket, besides, the cooler air soothes him."

They rocked in silence, until she said, "What's troubling you?"

He didn't know where to begin. When it came to spilling his guts…she was his baby sister and he didn't share his problems with her.

"You're in love with Isi," she said.

"How did you—"

"I guessed you were in love with her at Thanksgiving. You couldn't take your eyes off of her during dinner then you did everything possible to avoid her afterward. And when Will made a move on her playing football your skin actually turned green with jealousy."

"It did not," he said.

Dixie snorted. "You and Will had a tug-of-war match over Isi."

"You noticed, huh?"

"Noticed? You guys almost yanked the poor woman's arm off her body." Dixie smiled. "I was beginning to think she and Will had feelings for each other then she went off with you on a walk." She shifted Nate in her arms. "Is there some sort of love triangle going on between the three of you?"

"Isi told me she wanted to start dating and a coworker set her up with a guy who turned out to be a jerk so I said I'd find her a date."

"So you asked Will to take her out." Dixie chuckled.

"What's so funny?"

"You thought Will would be a safe date, didn't you?"

"Heck, yeah." Conway crossed his arms over his chest, not sure he liked opening up to his sister. "Will's older. Mature. He's not like younger guys who want jump into bed with—"

"Are you sure we're talking about the same brother?"

"What do you mean?"

"Will is all those things you said, but don't you remember he had a reputation in high school of being a bad boy?"

Conway thought back to those days and recalled his brother working three part-time jobs to save up enough money to buy a used Harley. The bike had been a babe magnet. "I forgot about the motorcycle."

"I can tell you from my observations on Thanksgiving that Isi only has eyes for you."

"She couldn't escape fast enough after dinner when she went into the house to help you with the dishes," Conway said.

"Men don't get it. If a woman loves a man that she knows she'll never have, she's not going to torment herself and allow the guy to keep coming around."

Was that why Isi told him to take the dog—because she'd been worried that he'd drop by the trailer to check on it?

"Isi's a nice girl, Conway, and her boys are cute."

Dixie sighed. "But you're not going to propose to her, are you?"

He shook his head.

"What are you afraid of?"

He'd never shared this story with any of his siblings—that he was willing to now, caught him off guard. "I think you were about fourteen when I found my father working as a ranch hand in northern Arizona."

"What's his name?"

"Zachary Johnson."

"I'm guessing your visit didn't go well, since you never mentioned it before now."

Conway shook his head. "He said he'd tried to do right by me and Mom but after six months he cut out on us, because he'd felt trapped by the responsibility of raising all of us."

"Did you ask him why he never visited you through the years?"

"He said he didn't know anything about being a father. His old man had cut out on him and his mother, too. And his grandfather had done the same to his wife and child."

"And you're afraid if you make a commitment to Isi, you'll end up running, too?"

That's exactly what he thought, but hearing Dixie say it out loud twisted his stomach into knots.

"What if you're nothing at all like your father?" she asked.

"Isi's sons have already been ditched by one father. It would be cruel if I married Isi then discovered I wasn't cut out to be a father and left her and the boys high and dry."

"Do you love Isi?" she asked.

"Yes."

"Then don't *try*—make it work."

"You're not listening to what I said."

"I heard you. Did your father say he loved Mom?"

Conway thought back on their conversation. "I don't think so." He doubted his father had loved anyone.

"When you love a person with all your heart, everything's on the table and everything's possible."

"What if I can't stick it out?"

"What if you can? What if you stay, and you turn out to be the best husband and father any wife and children could ask for? Are you willing to sacrifice your love for Isi, because you're afraid?"

Conway got up from the swing and walked to the end of the porch. "You make it sound simple."

"Give yourself credit, Conway. You're still here with the family."

"What do you mean?"

"If you were a cut-and-run guy, you would have left us long ago. But you stayed."

He'd never thought of it like that, but maybe his sister had a point.

"And you know why you didn't leave?"

"I'm sure you're dying to tell me," he said, flashing a smile.

"Because you love us and we love you."

Love. Was it possible that the four-letter word held more power over him than fear? "Miguel and Javier deserve a man who knows how to be a father. I've got no experience raising kids." Shoot, he'd already made the mistake of buying the boys a dog and then taking it away from them. And look at the trouble he'd caused when he'd given Javier advice about fighting—the kid had gotten suspended from school.

"You may share your father's genetics, but you also

share genes with your brothers and Grandpa Ely. All of them have taught you dedication, caring and responsibility."

What Dixie said made sense. Maybe the two genes would cancel each other out and Conway could start fresh and determine his own destiny.

"None of us had the best parents in the world, but I intend to love my son with everything inside me and hopefully my love will make up for my parenting mistakes."

"I want to believe love is enough." But he had an unproven track record.

"If your father would have apologized for abandoning you and asked for your forgiveness and an opportunity to be a part of your life, would you have given him a second chance?" Dixie asked.

Conway didn't have to think about his answer. "Yes." Having a father, no matter when he came along in his life, was something he'd always wished for.

"There's your answer, Conway. All a child really wants is to know they're loved and that their parents care what happens to them." Dixie smiled. "And you know what else?"

"What?"

"You already said you love Isi. Her sons are a part of her, so I know you love the boys, too."

He swallowed hard. Yes, he cared about Javier and Miguel. Cared about their feelings. Worried over them being bullied at school and wanted to keep them safe from harm. All that caring added up to love.

"The boys don't need a perfect father, Conway. They need a father to love them, faults and all, and not expect them to be *perfect*." She stroked the top of Nate's fuzzy head.

"I guess I have a lot to think about," he said.

"Where's Bandit?"

"Sleeping in the bunkhouse."

Dixie smiled as she shook her head.

"What now?"

"You determined your own destiny when you bought the dog."

"I'm not following."

"Whether you realized it or not, you bought that dog to tie Isi and the boys to you."

"You're crazy." His protest lacked conviction. He had been searching for a way to keep Isi in his life after he stopped babysitting the boys.

"Thanks for letting me bend your ear, Dix." His sister had given him much to ponder.

"I don't know if this will help you decide what to do about Isi, but now that Gavin and I are moving into Yuma, the farmhouse will be empty. Grandma Ada would want it to be filled with children again."

"Are you saying what I think you're saying?"

"I'm giving you first dibs on the house, but don't take long to decide. After watching one of those HGTV design shows, Porter's talking about making one of the bedrooms upstairs into a man cave."

"Porter needs to get a life."

Dixie laughed. "Conway."

"What?"

"Don't forget we're spending Christmas at the Triple D. We're supposed to be there by noon."

"I won't forget."

"THE LIGHTS ON that store are pretty," Isi said as she drove down a residential street Christmas Eve. The boys remained silent.

She felt like the Grinch. Her idea to drive through town and view holiday lights was a bust, and neither of her sons cared that Santa was coming tonight after they went to bed. The spirit had been sucked out of the holiday the moment she'd forced Conway to take Bandit home with him. Her life had been going along fine until that darn Bridget had broken her nose, then Isi's carefully controlled world had turned into...*fun*.

Conway had brought joy and laughter and good times into her and the boys' lives. Since the twins had been born, she'd worked hard to shelter them from the pain of their father's abandonment. Then Conway had crashed into their lives, showing her that she wasn't enough for her sons—they needed a father. A male role model. But before she'd had a chance to find that man her sons had formed an attachment to Conway and then he'd left them all with broken hearts.

Isi had allowed herself to get lost in the fantasy of being Conway's "the one" and she'd fallen in love with him, even knowing that he didn't want children. Her heart ached for the pouting boys in the backseat. She'd gladly sacrifice her own happiness to put smiles on their faces. Maybe she and Conway could share custody of Bandit. He could keep the dog during the week, and on weekends the puppy could live at the trailer.

Conway had made it clear he didn't want kids, but sharing a dog would keep him involved in the boys' lives. He wouldn't have any responsibility for them, but the twins could turn to him for advice about girls or guy troubles as they grew older.

What about you? How will you ever move on and find a man to love if Conway is always around reminding you that no other man will ever live up to him? She'd have to cross that bridge when she came to it.

"I was thinking," she said. "What if I talked to Conway about the possibility of sharing Bandit."

"How are we gonna share Bandit?" Miguel asked.

"After I begin my new job in January, I won't be working most weekends. Bandit could live with us on Saturday and Sunday and then stay at the farm during the week."

"I want Bandit to live with us all the time," Javier said.

"I know you do, honey, but both Conway and I told you that it wouldn't be fair to leave a dog like Bandit inside a trailer all day."

"What if Bandit wants to stay in our trailer?" Miguel asked.

If dogs could talk… "If you had a choice of running loose at the farm or being cooped up inside the trailer what would you choose?"

"The farm," Miguel said glumly.

"Should we ask Conway if Bandit could stay with us on the weekends?" She held her breath.

"Okay," Miguel said.

"What do you think, Javier?"

"Me, too. I want Bandit to stay with us."

"I'll call Conway after the holidays and discuss the idea with him." Isi turned into the trailer park.

"Mom, Conway's here!" Miguel unlocked his seat belt as she pulled beneath the carport. "Can we ask him now?"

Isi's heart pounded in her chest. What was Conway doing here on Christmas Eve?

"He brought Bandit, Mom!" Javier opened his door and the boys raced over to the porch where Conway sat with the dog. The puppy recognized the boys and barked a greeting.

"Hello, Conway." She stared at him, afraid if she blinked he'd vanish.

"I didn't know if you had plans Christmas Eve," he said.

"We were out looking at the holiday lights." Lord, he looked good tonight. She could smell his aftershave from five feet away and he'd pressed his jeans and Western shirt. She wondered what the special occasion was.

"I thought maybe you and the boys would like to spend Christmas Eve and Christmas Day at the farm with me and Bandit," he said.

Isi's first thought was the camera sitting on the kitchen counter. One more memory for the boys' scrapbooks—Christmas with Conway.

"Can we go, Mom?" Miguel begged.

"What about Santa?" She nibbled her lower lip. Even if the boys were on the fence about whether Santa Claus was real or not, she wanted to pretend at least for one more year.

"Santa stops at our farm," Conway said.

"Is there a place for the boys and me to sleep?" She'd like nothing more than to sleep in Conway's bed but that wasn't going to happen with all the Cash brothers sleeping in the bunkhouse.

"Dixie changed the sheets on the queen-size bed in the guest room and the boys and I can camp out in the yard." He grinned at the twins. "You guys ever sleep in a tent?"

Javier's eyes grew round. "What's a tent?"

"I guess that answers my question." Conway turned his brown eyes on Isi. "What do you say, Isi? Will you let us camp out tonight?"

Miguel and Javier tugged her hands and Bandit

jumped on her leg as if he was begging her to allow the boys to spend the night at the farm.

She had no idea what Conway's invitation meant, but she seized the opportunity to salvage the holiday for her sons. "Okay, we'll camp out at the farm."

The boys shouted and jumped for joy.

"I'll need to bring warm clothes and blankets," she said.

"We've got sleeping bags in the tent and extra pillows," Conway said. "The boys and I will stay out here and play with Bandit while you get their things together."

Taking her cue, Isi went inside and packed the boys' Christmas presents in a duffel bag then covered them with clothes. She threw in their teddy bears in case they got scared in the tent then added her makeup bag, toiletries and tooth brushes.

"All set?" Conway asked when she stepped outside.

"I think so. Boys, go use the bathroom before we head to the farm." Once the twins went inside, Isi said, "I'm sorry."

"For what?"

"For being such a grump about the dog." She smiled at Bandit who chewed on the tip of Conway's boot. "I told the boys that maybe you and I can work out a visitation schedule for Bandit so he can stay at the trailer on weekends."

Conway didn't make eye contact with her, and Isi sensed something troubled him. If they'd been at the bar, she would have asked him what was the matter, but after they'd slept together it wasn't the same between them. "If sharing Bandit is a hassle, I understand."

"We'll work it out." He stood when Miguel and Javier returned.

Isi smiled as she watched the boys play with the dog. Conway had been right to get them a companion—an animal that would love them unconditionally. If only she could find a man who loved her no matter what, too.

Five minutes later, Conway installed the booster seats in his truck and they piled in. The twins chatted the whole way to the farm with Bandit sleeping between them on the backseat.

CONWAY CLENCHED THE wheel tighter as he turned onto the road leading to the farmhouse. He was excited for the twins to see the Christmas tree he'd bought and strung lights on. Every kid deserved to find his presents from Santa beneath a real Christmas tree.

When he pulled into the yard, Javier shouted, "A Christmas tree!"

Standing in the middle of the yard was a twelve-foot spruce with twenty strings of colored lights wrapped around it. Conway had purchased extra extension cords and had plugged them into the outlets on the side of the bunkhouse. Right behind the tree was the tent he'd pitched earlier in the day.

As soon as he parked, the boys hopped out and raced to the tree, Bandit barking as he ran after them. Isi joined her sons and admired the spruce. "This is the most beautiful tree I've ever seen," she said.

The farmhouse door opened and Dixie and Gavin stepped outside. "Merry Christmas, everyone!" Dixie called.

Gavin and Dixie joined Conway and Isi in front of the tree. "Conway was out here all day stringing those lights," Gavin said.

"I've never seen a tree with so many lights." She smiled at Conway. "The branches are hardly visible."

The bunkhouse door banged open. Buck, Porter, Mack and Will walked out wearing Santa hats, Mack strumming his guitar. Bandit ran toward the Cash brothers and Miguel and Javier chased after the dog.

"Where's the hot chocolate?" Mack asked.

"I'll make it right now." Dixie took Isi's hand. "Would you help me inside? I've got cookies in the oven."

After Isi and Dixie went into the house, Miguel tugged on Conway's hand. "Can Javi and I take Bandit into the tent?"

"Sure, but don't let Bandit do his job in there," Conway said.

As soon as the boys were out of earshot, Will spoke. "Are you getting cold feet?"

"No way. I'm ready." Nothing had ever felt as right as wanting to ask Isi to marry him.

Porter jabbed his elbow in Mack's side and whispered. "I told you Conway was serious about proposing to her."

With Dixie's help, Conway had set the scene for his wedding proposal. He wanted his siblings to be present when he asked the most important question of his life. Conway had hoped if Isi had any doubts, his brothers would vouch for him. "Where's Johnny?" he asked his brothers.

"Looks like he's coming right now." Porter pointed to the lights cutting through the trees on the road leading to the farmhouse.

Johnny parked his pickup next to the other vehicles in the yard. He and Shannon got out and joined them in front of the tree.

"Conway, the tree is beautiful." Shannon slipped her arm through Johnny's and said, "Next year we should use colored lights instead of white ones on our tree."

"Colored lights are more for kids than adults," Johnny said.

"Exactly." Shannon ignored Johnny's perplexed frown and moved closer to the tree.

"You have the ring?" Buck asked.

Conway patted his pants pocket. "Right here." He could only afford a small diamond and he hoped Isi wouldn't mind that she wasn't getting a rock like the diamond Gavin had picked out for Dixie.

A few minutes later, Dixie and Isi came outside with a pitcher of hot chocolate, plastic cups and a plate of cookies.

The boys came out of the tent and joined the adults. While everyone drank cocoa and ate cookies, Conway rehearsed in his mind what he wanted to say but he kept getting confused and mixing up his sentences. In the end, he gave up because there were no words to convey his love for Isi. After a few minutes, conversation died down and Dixie looked expectantly at him.

Porter cleared his throat.

Mack strummed a chord on his guitar.

Buck grinned.

Will winked at Isi.

And when Johnny made eye contact with him and nodded, Conway knew he was ready.

"What's going on?" Isi glanced between Conway and his siblings.

Dixie handed the pitcher to Gavin then herded the twins closer to Isi.

Conway dropped to one knee in front of them and took Isi's left hand in his. Her eyes grew round.

Keep it short and simple and don't screw up.

"Isi, I know you can do better than me, but you're 'the one' and you've been right in front of me for two years

I love you and—" he smiled at the boys "—I love Javi and Mig. Will the three of you marry me?"

Tears leaked from Isi's eyes. "Are you sure, Conway?"

He dug the ring out of his pants' pocket. "This is how sure I am." He slid the diamond over her finger then stood.

Isi flung herself at Conway. "Yes, I'll marry you." After a heated kiss she said, "I fell in love with you a long time ago when you first walked into the bar and swept me off my feet."

Conway turned to the twins. "Boys, I'd sure like to be your dad. Will you let me?"

Javier stepped forward and buried his face against Conway's thigh. Miguel offered Conway a high five then chased Bandit, shouting, "Conway Twitty Cash is gonna be my dad! Conway Twitty Cash is gonna be my dad!"

The adults laughed and offered their congratulations. Then Conway pulled Isi close and whispered, "I've been dying to kiss you forever." The kiss was slow and sweet and everything Conway had dreamed it would be.

When the kiss ended, Isi whispered in his ear, "I promise I'll love you so much and so hard for the rest of my life that you'll never want to leave me or the boys."

Conway closed his eyes, his throat thickening with emotion. "I'm going to hold you to that promise, Isi, because there's nowhere else I'd rather be than with the three of you."

Mack strummed his guitar. "I'm taking requests."

Isi smiled at Conway and said, "I've Already Loved You In My Mind."

Conway was familiar with the song about a guy who meets a girl in a bar. He pulled Isi into his arms and they slowed danced in front of the Christmas tree while Mack's baritone voice serenaded them. Dixie and Gavin joined the dancing couple then Johnny and Shannon. Porter grabbed Miguel and danced with him and Buck twirled Javier.

"How did I get stuck dancing with the dog?" Will laughed and picked up Bandit.

"I'll never forget this Christmas, Conway." Isi snuggled closer.

Neither would he, because tonight marked the end of the long line of cut-and-run cowboys he'd descended from.

CHRISTMAS DAY AT the Triple D was unlike anything Isi had ever experienced. The scent of fresh-cut evergreen, cinnamon and roasting turkey filled the ranch house. An eight-foot evergreen with twinkling white lights stood in the corner of the living room and presents wrapped in shiny red paper rested beneath its branches—mostly gifts for Javier and Miguel and Dixie's son, Nathan. Isi was overwhelmed by the Cash family's generosity toward her and her sons.

Her heart burst with joy and happiness as she watched Javi and Mig open their gifts from Johnny and Shannon. A squawk drew her attention to Nate. Drool hanging from his mouth, the baby sat on his uncle Mack's knee, watching the twins tear at the wrapping paper. Out of the corner of her eye, Isi saw Dixie maneuver Gavin beneath a sprig of mistletoe and kiss him. Fiona Wilson slipped her hand through Clive Douglas's as they stood in front of the fireplace and watched the group. Shannon's brothers Luke and Matt regaled Porter, Buck and Will with humorous stories of their lates court trial, while Shannon snuggled in Johnny's arms next to the tree.

"The family can be overwhelming until you get used to them." Conway wrapped his arm around her waist.

"I love your family." She wiped at a tear.

"Why are you crying?"

"I wish my parents and brothers could see how happy you've made me and the boys."

"I'd like to believe they know how happy we are," he said.

She hugged Conway then pulled away when Dixie approached and handed her a gift.

Embarrassed, Isi said, "I didn't know we were exchanging gifts."

"We're not," Dixie said. "It's a welcome-to-the-family present. Open it."

Isi peeled off the candy-cane paper and removed the lid on the box. A set of shiny keys rested on a bed of cotton. "Do you know what these are for?" Isi asked Conway.

He nodded but Dixie explained. "Gavin and I closed on our new house in Yuma and we're moving in two weeks. I want you, Conway and the boys to live in the farmhouse."

Isi pressed a hand to her thumping heart. "Shouldn't your brothers have first dibs on the house?"

"Grandma Ada always said that a farmhouse was meant to be filled with children and I could tell how much you loved the place when you came for Thanksgiving." Dixie squeezed Isi's hand. "My grandmother would be thrilled to know the house is in your loving hands and that Javier and Miguel's laughter will fill the rooms."

"I don't know what to say." Isi forced the words past the lump in her throat.

"Say yes to the house, Isi," Conway said.

"Yes!" Isi hugged Dixie.

"I'd like to make an announcement," Shannon said.

The chatter stopped and everyone's attention turned to Shannon. "First, I'd like to apologize to my husband for being in such a bad mood the past few weeks. I'm afraid my emotions have been off-kilter since…" Shannon smiled at Johnny. "I found out I'm pregnant."

Johnny's mouth sagged.

"Well hot dang, we got ourselves another baby coming in the family," Porter said.

"Who's having a baby?" Miguel asked.

"Aunt Shannon." Dixie crossed the room to hug her best friend.

"Is it a girl baby or a boy baby?" Javier asked.

"I don't know, Javi." Shannon smiled at her stunned husband. "We won't find out until next June."

Shannon's father hugged her. "Congratulations, daughter. Regardless if it's a girl or a boy, I suspect we'll have another bull rider in the family."

"That'll give Johnny more gray hair," Porter said.

Conway laughed. "Hey, big brother. You gonna just stand there with your jaw scraping the floor or are you going to kiss your wife?"

Johnny took Shannon in his arms and kissed her while the rest of the Cash clan hollered encouragement.

"I'd like to propose a toast." Will held up his beer bottle. "To Conway and Isi—may you always find happiness in each other's arms and to Shannon—thank you for giving our brother his own kid to worry about, so he'll stop sticking his nose in our business."

Laughter and ribbing followed Will's statement. Is

tapped her wineglass against Conway's beer bottle. In the future, maybe they'd add a second set of twins to their little family, but if not, she'd still be the happiest woman alive, because Conway had given her a dream come true—a father for her sons and her very own happy ever after.

* * * * *

Be sure to look for the next book by Marin Thomas featuring the Cash Brothers available in 2014!

REQUEST YOUR FREE BOOKS!
2 FREE NOVELS PLUS 2 FREE GIFTS!

⊕ HARLEQUIN®

American ★ Romance®

LOVE, HOME & HAPPINESS

YES! Please send me 2 FREE Harlequin® American Romance® novels and my 2 FREE gifts (gifts are worth about $10). After receiving them, if I don't wish to receive any more books, I can return the shipping statement marked "cancel." If I don't cancel, I will receive 4 brand-new novels every month and be billed just $4.74 per book in the U.S. or $5.24 per book in Canada. That's a savings of at least 14% off the cover price! It's quite a bargain! Shipping and handling is just 50¢ per book in the U.S. and 75¢ per book in Canada.* I understand that accepting the 2 free books and gifts places me under no obligation to buy anything. I can always return a shipment and cancel at any time. Even if I never buy another book, the two free books and gifts are mine to keep forever.

154/354 HDN F4YN

Name	(PLEASE PRINT)

Address	Apt. #

City	State/Prov.	Zip/Postal Code

Signature (if under 18, a parent or guardian must sign)

Mail to the **Harlequin® Reader Service:**
IN U.S.A.: P.O. Box 1867, Buffalo, NY 14240-1867
IN CANADA: P.O. Box 609, Fort Erie, Ontario L2A 5X3

Want to try two free books from another line?
Call 1-800-873-8635 or visit www.ReaderService.com.

* Terms and prices subject to change without notice. Prices do not include applicable taxes. Sales tax applicable in N.Y. Canadian residents will be charged applicable taxes. Offer not valid in Quebec. This offer is limited to one order per household. Not valid for current subscribers to Harlequin American Romance books. All orders subject to credit approval. Credit or debit balances in a customer's account(s) may be offset by any other outstanding balance owed by or to the customer. Please allow 4 to 6 weeks for delivery. Offer available while quantities last.

Your Privacy—The Harlequin® Reader Service is committed to protecting your privacy. Our Privacy Policy is available online at www.ReaderService.com or upon request from the Harlequin Reader Service.

We make a portion of our mailing list available to reputable third parties that offer products we believe may interest you. If you prefer that we not exchange your name with third parties, or if you wish to clarify or modify your communication preferences, please visit us at www.ReaderService.com/consumerchoice or write to us at Harlequin Reader Service Preference Service, P.O. Box 9062, Buffalo, NY 14269. Include your complete name and address.

HAR13R

SPECIAL EXCERPT FROM

H HARLEQUIN®

American Romance®

Read on for a sneak peek at
HIS CHRISTMAS SWEETHEART
by New York Times *bestselling author*
Cathy McDavid

The handsome ranch hand Will Desarro is a man of few
words, but Miranda Staley soon discovers that beneath
that quiet exterior beats a heart of gold.

Miranda grinned. Will Dessaro was absolutely adorable
when flustered—and he was flustered a lot around her.

How had she coexisted in the same town with him for all
these years and not noticed him?

Then came the day of the fire and the order to evacuate
within two hours. He'd shown up on her doorstep, strong,
silent, capable, and provided the help she'd needed to rally
and load her five frightened and uncooperative residents
into the van.

She couldn't have done it without him. And he'd been
visiting Mrs. Litey regularly ever since.

Thank the Lord her house had been spared. The same
couldn't be said for several hundred other homes and build-
ings in Sweetheart, including many on her own street. Her
beautiful and quaint hometown had been brought to its
knees in a matter of hours and still hadn't recovered five
months later.

"I hate to impose…." Miranda glanced over her shoulder,
making sure Will had accompanied her into the kitchen.
"There's a leak in the pipe under the sink. The repairman
can't fit me in his schedule till Monday, and the leak

worsening by the hour." She paused. "You're good with tools, aren't you?"

"Good enough." He blushed.

Sweet heaven, he was a cutie.

Wavy brown hair that insisted on falling rakishly over one brow. Dark eyes. Cleft in his chin. Breathtakingly tall. He towered above her five-foot-three frame.

If only he'd respond to one of the many dozen hints she'd dropped and ask her on a date.

"Do you mind taking a peek for me?" She gestured toward the open cabinet doors beneath the sink. "I'd really appreciate it."

"Sure." His gaze went to the toolbox on the floor. "You have an old towel or pillow I can use?"

That had to be the longest sentence he'd ever uttered in her presence.

"Be right back." She returned shortly with an old beach towel folded in a large square.

By then, Will had set his cowboy hat on the table and rolled up his sleeves.

Nice arms, she noted. Tanned, lightly dusted with hair and corded with muscles.

She flashed him another brilliant smile and handed him the towel.

His blush deepened.

Excellent. Message sent and received.

Will Miranda lasso her shy cowboy this holiday season?
Find out in
HIS CHRISTMAS SWEETHEART
by New York Times *bestselling author Cathy McDavid*
Available November 5, 2013,
only from Harlequin® American Romance®.

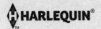

American Romance®

To Love, Honor…and Multiply!

Becoming a husband and family man in the middle of a raging land feud wasn't the destiny Galen Callahan saw for himself. But once he laid eyes on Rose Carstairs, he knew the bouncy blonde with the warrior heart was his future. Now, with Rancho Diablo under siege, the eldest Callahan sibling will do whatever it takes to protect his new wife and triplets. With Callahan lives and legacy on the line, Galen has a new mission: to vanquish a dangerous enemy and bring his family together in time for Christmas!

A *Callahan Christmas Miracle*
by *USA TODAY* bestselling author
TINA LEONARD

**Available November 5,
from Harlequin® American Romance®.**